Dak's Omega

A Bear's Cove Novel

by

A·J· Stone

Bear's Cove 1: Dak's Omega
Copyright © March 2018 by A.J. Stone
Print ISBN: 978-1-942414-55-1

Editor: Nicoline Tiernan
Cover Artist: Anne Kay

Published by Lost Goddess Publishing LLC

Warning: This book contains sexually explicit scenes and adult language and may be considered offensive to some readers. It is not meant for underage readers.

Bear's Cove is Dak Freeman's chance to start over.
Leaving Forrest Hills and his ex-husband behind, Dak vowed to start over as a deputy in the small, bear-shifter town of Bear's Cove. On his two first nights, he's called to a nightclub to restore order. Both times, handsome Chase Longfellow is the one causing problems.

Chase Longfellow had been an outcast his whole life.
Waking up in a jail cell wasn't a new experience for Chase, and this time was more fun because it afforded him a chance to flirt with the virile new alpha Daddy on the other side of the bars.

Dak's alpha nature means he can't help but take the wayward cub in hand, and when the omega responds to his dominance, Dak's fractured heart begins to heal.
A passionate night leaves Chase pregnant, but when Dak's ex returns and tragedy strikes, everything is threatened. Is their new love strong enough to survive?

Welcome to Bear's Cove, a hidden community of gay bear shifters. Dak's Omega is a 32,000-word, gay male pregnancy romance that includes passionate and explicit sexual content, including bondage, Daddy/cub dynamic, and violence, suitable for adult audiences.

Prologue

"You're taking this awfully well." Abe Freeman discarded a four and took his chances with a new card.

Dak Freeman stared at the four, concentrating hard. He had a four in his hand already, as well as a pair of threes. Should he take a chance with these low cards or hold out for something better? A bark of laughter burst from him as he realized this question exemplified his life choices.

His father's question nagged at the part of him trying not to be angry. "Dad's in there, supervising and helping."

Abe chuffed, showing his disapproval and his inner bear. "This isn't right, Dak. When we chose Hoyt for you, the Grazianos promised he was loyal and eager."

Ten years ago, when they'd been seventeen, Dak's fathers and Hoyt's parents had arranged their marriage. Unlike many of the bears their age, neither man had protested. The betrothal period lasted four years, and six years ago, Dak had wed Hoyt.

And now Hoyt was moving out. Though they got along, their marriage lacked excitement. Dak wanted children, and Hoyt wanted adventure.

"Your heart is broken," Abe said. "I know my son. I know you're upset."

Dak was angry, not heartbroken, which probably proved Hoyt's assertion they weren't in love with each other. Dak's alpha nature had been more affected than his heart. He picked up the four. Old habits died hard. "I'm fine, Papa. You and Dad need looking after. This will give me more time with you. The nurse won't need to stop by every day."

The Freemans loved to scavenge for fresh kills, often finishing off whatever wolf shifters left behind. Two seasons ago, they'd contracted a nasty virus that ravaged their immune systems. Some days they had energy, and other times they didn't. A nurse came to see them every day, as did Dak. He didn't mind caring for his fathers, two men he loved and admired, and with his three brothers scattered across the country, they needed him here.

Abe frowned, a severe expression of displeasure. "You're not going to bury yourself here, working and taking care of us. You need to get out of Forrest Hills. A change of scenery will do you good."

Outside, car doors slammed. Desmond, Dak's other father, spoke. Dak heard his voice, but he couldn't make out any words.

Abe discarded a ten of hearts. "We made arrangements with Chad Bearsmith's son, Cord, for a job in Bear's Cove."

Bear's Cove was a four-hour drive southeast, a tiny fishing hamlet nestled along the coast. Forrest Hills was Dak's home. Though his brothers had gone, he'd never once thought about leaving the place where his beloved parents had raised them and still lived.

"I don't want to leave. In a couple years, Sheriff Trapper will retire, and I'll get that post." Right now, Dak worked at a local fishery. It left him with time to nurse his fathers and go hunting in the heavily wooded mountainside whenever the whim struck.

Abe put a hand over Dak's. "Son, Papa and I are fine. The worst is over for us. We're on the mend."

"Doctors said it would take at least another six months of therapy before they knew anything."

"And yet, the worst is over." Steel reinforced Abe's clear blue eyes, so like Dak's. "You need to focus on yourself, Dak. You need to get on with your life. Start over."

Start over in a town four hours away he'd visited a few times. As a homebody, Dak didn't want to leave. But he wanted to fall in love and have a family. That wasn't going to happen if he remained in Forrest Hills. In this small community, everyone knew his business, and everyone knew he'd failed. Besides, there was nobody around he cared to date.

Perhaps his dad was right—he needed a change of scenery. If the doctor said they were on the mend, then that was one worry Dak no longer had.

He could rent a place for six months and see how he liked it.

Though Dak also had a ten in his hand, he picked up from the dealer's stack. "Okay, Dad. You win. I'll give Bear's Cove a try."

Chapter One

"I dare you."

Chase Longfellow eyed the ten shots lined up on the bar, and then he shot a grin at his best friend, Logan Fordline. "A hundred bucks." Confident he'd win the bet, he held out a hand for the money.

Logan shook his head. "I know better than to pay you ahead of time. Drink up, party boy."

Never one to turn down a drink or a bet, Chase slammed the first shot of whiskey. Before it burned a line down the inside of his chest, he downed the next four.

The crowd around the bar grew thicker, and a cadre of men chanted for him to keep it up.

In his element, Chase's grin grew even though it was hard to smile and drink. After the tenth shot, he pumped a fist in the air and let loose with an ear-splitting whoop.

Logan clapped him on the back and slapped five twenties on the bar. "You're crazy, man. Crazy."

Chase stuffed the wad of cash into his pocket and pulled Logan onto the dance floor. In seconds, bodies surrounded them. A solid chest pressed into Chase's back, and strong hands staked a claim on his hips, holding him close. Looking back over his shoulder, Chase recognized Manatee Thompson, a bear of a man who'd tried a few times to convince him to come home for a one-night stand.

While Chase was all for a one-off bout of sex, he wasn't attracted to Manatee. The man was tall and built, but his scent didn't stir Chase's libido. Still he was fun to dance with. Chase thrust his ass back and ground it against Manatee's groin.

Music pulsed, colored lights swept the room, and Chase gave himself over to the beat. He abandoned Manatee to press his body to various others, not noticing or caring who they were. The alcohol had hit his system, and he barely remembered what Logan looked like.

Someone grabbed his hand. "Let's go up to the roof."

That sounded like a great idea. The club had become too hot anyway. "Fun!" Chase followed along, letting the hand pull him through a door that warned the area was off-limits.

He had no idea who he was with, and he didn't care. The guy seemed familiar, and he wanted to party, so Chase was fine with it.

They climbed a staircase and emerged on a flat roof. City lights blinked around them, mostly streetlights because the office buildings were closed up for the night.

Chase stood near the edge and swayed. "It's fucking beautiful."

The guy laughed, the noise grating like a hyena shifter.

"What's your name?"

"Albert."

"I'm Chase."

Albert's laugh came harder. "I know, dumbass. We went to high school together."

Vague memories surfaced. High school had ended five years ago, so even when sober, it wasn't fresh in his memory. He forced his inebriated brain to focus on Albert. They were about the same height, but where Chase had a lanky build, Albert had filled out. Chase was clean-shaven, and Albert sported a manicured beard.

By way of explaining the lack of recognition, Chase hiccupped. "I'm drunk."

"So am I." Albert laughed again, and he motioned to empty beer bottles someone had abandoned nearby. "Let's see how far we can throw those."

It sounded like a great idea. Chase picked one up and hurled it with all his might. The dark brown bottle glinted in the bright fluorescent lights in the parking lot as it tumbled end-over-end. It landed with a crash, shattering on the asphalt next to a parked car.

Albert jumped up and down. "That was fucking fantastic." He threw the next one. It didn't go as far as Chase's had, and it landed in the back of a pickup truck where it bounced around without breaking.

Chase tried to admire the skill of the throw with a low whistle, but his lips were numb. "Let's see how many we can get in the back of the truck." It was like basketball with beer bottles and a stranger's truck bed.

The two of them made short work of the stash, and then they went looking for more bottles. Albert sniffed out a few on the other side of the roof. Rather than take them back to their original spot, they chose a new target.

Albert threw the first one, and it hit the windshield of a vehicle parked in the street. Cracks spiderwebbed outward from the point of impact.

Albert smacked a hand over his mouth. "Oh, fuck me raw. Let's get out of here."

Chase's brain wasn't working so well. He stared at the windshield, wondering what the hell was going on. Sirens sounded in the distance,

4

coming ever closer. They stopped below him, the red and blue lights hypnotizing him with the way they spun around, throwing light and shadows in dizzying circles.

"Hands in the air."

The command came from behind him, the authoritative voice sending a primal thrill that traveled a direct route to Chase's core. He shivered and turned to find a flashlight shining directly into his eyes.

Wincing, he averted his gaze. "Dude, don't be a dick."

"Were you throwing beer bottles off the roof?"

Some instinct warned him that a positive response wouldn't be in his best interest. He had no trouble pasting on a puzzled expression. "Who are you?" Though he knew the sheriff and all the deputies, he couldn't make out any features of the man on the other side of the light.

"Deputy Freeman."

That wasn't a familiar name. Chase swayed. "Hi, Deputy. Can I call you Dep?" He giggled at his own joke.

The light lowered a bit. Once his eyes adjusted to the normal bleariness that went with his level of drunkness, Chase's breath caught. Deputy Freeman was a big man in all the right ways. His jacket draped over broad shoulders. It hid a lot, but not those trim hips or powerful thighs. Though he couldn't quite focus, Chase thought he detected blue eyes glaring at him from under a shock of rich brown hair. Everything about the Deputy exuded strength, power, and control.

This was a man who might have a beer at the end of the day, but who never, ever drank to excess.

"You're drunk."

Chase tried to nod, but the world swam out of focus, so he stopped. "Yep."

"Were you throwing bottles off the roof?"

Again, that shred of self-preservation prevented him from responding. "Dep-you-tee, you are so fucking hot. Maybe you should take off your jacket?" Chase took one step closer, but he tripped over nothing, sending his body headlong into the Deputy's.

Freeman caught him.

Looking up at his savior, Chase drowned in those blue pools for five whole seconds before the world swam out of focus.

Chapter Two

Dak Freeman set the young man's body on the surface of the roof and sighed. First day on the job, and he was already collecting for the drunk tank. He got on his radio. "This is Freeman. I'm bringing in one to sleep it off."

He didn't know if this cub was responsible for the broken windshield or the shards of glass littering the parking lot, but he was willing to lay odds on it. Lacking another option, he scooped up the unconscious man and carried him down the stairs.

The owner of the bar, Cameron Houser, waited at the foot of the steps. "I saw him go up there earlier."

Hovering in the background, a man who looked a lot like Houser blushed and averted his gaze.

He smelled guilty. More than that, his scent was on the man in his arms. Dak seized on this. "You were up there with him."

The man shrugged. "Maybe."

Houser whirled. "You took him up to the roof? What the hell is wrong with you?"

"It was harmless fun." The boy didn't appear concerned.

His father was having none of it. "Albert, it wasn't harmless fun. You will pay for that windshield, and you will clean up the parking lot. Grab a broom."

Albert huffed out his chagrin, but he scurried off to follow his father's command.

Houser turned to Dak. "I'm not pressing charges."

Dak shifted the man in his arms. The man's slim build didn't strain his muscles, but his potent scent stirred a longing Dak would rather stay dormant. "What's his name?"

"Chase Longfellow. He's harmless."

"He was served too much alcohol." Dak growled. Though he was well within his rights as a protector of the citizens of Bear's Cove to be upset about someone being served too much, that wasn't the reason his hackles had been raised. There was something about this man, a pheromone maybe, that made Dak hold him a little closer.

"Yeah." Cameron sniffed, his nose twitching. "He'll be okay. He just needs to sleep it off."

Dak nodded. "I'll take him out the back way." Without waiting for a reply, he left. His acute sense of smell told him the same thing

Cameron Houser had—this cub was going to wake up with one hell of a headache.

When the call from dispatch had come in, Dak had eagerly set out to bring in a drunk-and-disorderly—his first real arrest. He looked forward to processing the paperwork and recommending charges to the prosecutor's office.

But one look at the man swaying dangerously close to the low wall on the flat roof of the only nightclub in town, and Dak's better sense had fled, taking protocol along for the ride.

Dak loaded Chase into the back of his patrol car. Then he settled into the driver's seat and called in his location. "Dispatch, this is Freeman. Houser declined to press charges. I'm going to call it a night and head home."

"Dispatch here. What about the deposit for the drunk tank?" Cord Bearsmith's voice crackled over the radio. Bearsmith filled multiple roles in the small outpost—they all did—and tonight the Sheriff manned the phones.

"Negative on that. I'll drop him home."

"Roger that. Dispatch out."

Having Chase's name meant Dak could look him up in the database, but he decided against it. Instead, he took Chase to his house. The cub didn't rouse as Dak deposited him on the sofa.

Dak stepped back to look over his charge. He was young, perhaps five or six years younger than Dak. Blond hair fell over his face, accenting the sharp cheekbones and the aquiline nose. His oval face terminated in a pointed chin, giving the cub an impish look.

A cotton shirt covered his torso, but it had ridden up a bit to reveal a defined strip of abdomen with a thin line of light hair leading into the younger man's jeans. Dak's gaze followed the denim down, noting the man was a little too long for the sofa. His large feet dangled off the edge. Lean and lithe, this man was exactly Dak's type.

Chase Longfellow was one handsome shifter.

One drunken, irresponsible, utterly sexy cub in need of someone to whip his ass into shape.

Dak didn't make the mistake of thinking he was that man. Cord had taken a chance on hiring him—a law-enforcement officer with almost no practical experience—and he wasn't going to let his new friend down by getting involved with the wrong sort of bear.

Seeing as how he had an inebriated stranger—no matter how sexy—in his house, he kept the bedroom door open while he slept.

A crash and liberal swearing woke him before his alarm had that pleasure. Light streaked through the window. Instantly alert, Dak leapt from bed and shifted into his bear form.

He lumbered into the living room to find Chase sprawled on the floor, one leg of his jeans turned inside out but still clinging to his calf and covering his foot.

The cub stopped kicking his legs long enough to look up. Eyes wide and disbelieving, he held up a hand. "Whoa—who the fuck are you? Where am I?"

Seeing as how there was no immediate danger, Dak shifted back into human form. He parked his hands on his hips and regarded the man on his floor. "Deputy Dak Freeman. What are you doing?"

Chase looked around, blinking as if he was still waking up from a deep sleep. "Deputy? Did you arrest me? This doesn't look like jail."

Dak headed back to the bedroom for some clothes. Shifting left one naked, and being clothed was an armor he needed against the vision of sex incarnate on his living room floor. It was going to be difficult to maintain his position of authority while his morning wood made eyes at Chase Longfellow.

As he shoved his long legs into sweats, he heard sounds of water in the bathroom. With a grunt, he slid a shirt over his head and went to the kitchen. When Chase came out of the bathroom, Dak handed him an aspirin and a glass of orange juice.

Chase gulped both down without comment, but his puzzled and distrustful gaze never left Dak's face.

Dak held out a hand for the empty glass. "Get your shoes on. I'm taking you home."

The cub responded to Dak's authoritative tone—or maybe he just wanted to go home. Either way, he laced up his tennis shoes. Then he looked around. "Where's my jacket?"

Dak shrugged. "This is all you had when you passed out. I would have taken you home, but you weren't in a position to tell me where you live." He snagged his keys and motioned to the door. "What's your address, cub?"

At the door, Chase whirled. He stared straight into Dak's eyes. "Cub? I'm a full grown bear, and I'd appreciate if you treated me as such."

Grabbing the smaller man by the scruff, Dak hauled him out the door and to the patrol car. He tossed the cub into the back seat. "You act like a mature bear, I'll treat you like a mature bear. You drink until you pass out, and I'll treat you like the dumbass cub you are."

In the rearview mirror, Dak watched Chase cross his arms and flop back against the seat. His lush bottom lip pushed out in a pout. "I need to get my jacket. It has my keys in it. I can't get into my house without my keys."

Ten minutes later, Dak pounded on the nightclub's door. The Bear's Den had been a staple of the town for as long as anybody could remember. Most days it was a sedate bar where a bear could enjoy a beer while watching TV. Friday and Saturday nights, it was a nightclub that catered to the younger crowd.

Dak wasn't old, but he'd never really gone in for loud, pulsating music and a throng of sweaty bodies. Maybe he just had an old soul.

Nobody answered the door.

Next to him, Chase glanced around the parking lot.

"Looking for broken glass to clean up?"

Chase started. "Excuse me?"

"Broken glass." Dak frowned at Chase. "You and Albert Houser were throwing beer bottles off the roof last night. You broke a truck's windshield and made one hell of a mess in the parking lot. That's why I picked you up last night. Houser declined to press charges. The truck was his."

Chase's nose scrunched, drawing attention to his rich brown eyes. "I was hanging out with Albert Houser and I don't remember a single moment? Damn. He used to be so hot. I had a crush on him in high school. I was a freshman when he was a senior, and he never looked my way."

Rather than listen to him reminisce about guys he'd lusted after, Dak hammered at the door again. "I don't think anyone is here."

Chase stepped back and peered upward as if someone was going to peek over the edge of the roof. "I know where they live."

It looked like he had no choice. Dak drove Chase to the Houser's residence. This time, he let Chase ride in the front seat.

Bouncing around exuberantly, Chase reached for the dials on the radio.

Dak smacked his hand away. "No touching anything, or you're going in the back seat."

That pout reappeared, but this time it was more cute than bratty. "You're no fun, Deputy Bossypants."

"None," he agreed. "I'm driving around an irresponsible cub on my morning off instead of sleeping in and having a huge breakfast."

Chase reached over and set a hand on Dak's arm. "Let me buy you breakfast."

Dak frowned. Without taking his gaze from the road, he managed to convey doubt. "How are you going to pay for it? Isn't your wallet in your jacket?"

"Doesn't matter." He patted his jean's pocket. "I have cash. Come on, let me buy you breakfast. You can scowl at me across the table while you lecture me about my irresponsible ways."

As tempting as that sounded, Dak wasn't inclined to agree. He mustered his resolve. "No, thanks."

"Come on." Chase walked two fingers up Dak's arm, sending pleasant tingles in all directions. "How about a drive thru? I bet you're not so growly after you've eaten."

Just then, Dak's stomach let loose with a loud rumble. He turned into the first open fast food place. "Fine. What do you want?"

With a grin that seemed impossible for someone who should have a splitting headache, Chase ordered an impressive amount of food.

Bears were big eaters, and bear shifters required even more energy to keep them going—especially in cooler weather when they all fought the natural urge to hibernate.

Fortified with greasy eggs and hash browns, Dak continued to the Houser residence. Cameron wasn't pleased to see them.

"It's nine o'clock in the morning, Deputy." He shot a suspicious look in Chase's direction. "And I don't remember Cord ever chauffeuring around a drunk."

Dak refrained from responding. His features remained impassive even though he was tempted to grunt a warning.

"Dad? Is that Chase?" Albert appeared behind his father. Shirtless, barefoot, and grinning, he held a jacket aloft. He slid past his father and Dak, coming to a halt in front of Chase. "I was going to come down and bail you out this morning." He followed up with a teasing grin while he dragged a fingertip down the front of Chase's chest.

Dak rolled his eyes. "You want me to leave you here, party boy, or take you home?" He couldn't keep the note of irritation from creeping into his tone. Who the fuck did this cub think he was putting his hands on Dak's...what?

Chase didn't belong to Dak. He might be a cub, but he wasn't Dak's cub. Not a half hour ago, Chase had confessed to having a crush on Albert. So Dak reined in the primal possessiveness threatening to overtake him.

The younger man's gaze flickered to Dak and back to Albert. His pink tongue darted out to wet his lower lip. He flashed a disarming smile at Albert as he accepted custody of his jacket. "Thanks for hanging onto this. I have to get home."

The smallest bit of tension drained from Dak's shoulders, though he remained on full alert. Something about this bear—his scent, his sexy body, his graceful bearing—called to a place inside Dak he hadn't known existed.

Back in the car, Dak entered Chase's address into the car's computer. He said nothing as he drove to the other end of town, but thoughts ricocheted through his brain enough to give him the beginnings of a headache.

He had no business being attracted to a man like Chase Longfellow. Everything about him was wrong—from his carefree demeanor to the way he shamelessly flirted with everyone. Okay, maybe he'd only flirted with Albert, but it was enough to reinforce the notion that Dak was not on Chase's radar.

Bringing the cruiser to a halt at the address, Dak didn't look at his charge. "If there's a next time, I'll arrest your ass."

Chase paused with his hand on the latch. "Threatening me with handcuffs? I think I like it."

Too shocked to maintain his gruff, impassive exterior, Dak glanced over to see Chase regarding him with an impish grin. The cub winked as he exited the car.

Dak watched him go, noting the way Chase's jeans hugged that tight ass.

Chapter Three

Without glancing back, Chase added a little swagger to his step. He knew that Deputy Hardass was watching him walk up the path to the front door, and he wanted to make it worth his while.

Waking up in a strange place was nothing new for Chase. He'd been surprised to find himself fully clothed, which wasn't a great thing when a night of drinking meant he really needed the bathroom.

Fumbling with his jeans, he'd tripped over a cord running across the floor that led to a laptop sitting on the low table in front of the sofa. He'd failed to notice either thing.

And then he'd looked up to find a large black bear approaching. For a second, he'd panicked, and then he'd recognized those clear blue eyes, but the memory had a dreamlike quality. Dak's story about picking him up was probably true.

But why had he taken Chase to his house instead of letting him sleep it off in the jail?

Chase knew he was handsome and in peak physical shape. His whole life, it had been easy to charm anyone and everyone with a smile, benign flirting, or even a sexy pout. None of those weapons had worked on the mysterious new deputy whose face hadn't hinted at any kind of reaction.

It only made Chase determined to get a rise out of the man in blue.

Sliding the key into the keyhole, Chase smiled. "Eat your heart out, Deputy Dak Freeman."

He opened the door to find his grandmother sitting in her recliner with a clear view to the door. Mentally, he cursed. "Grandma, I told you not to wait up for me."

She lowered the footrest and rubbed her eyes. "Asking me to stop worrying about you is asking me to stop loving you. It's impossible."

Chase helped her get out of the comfortable chair. He waited while her legs steadied. Simone Longfellow was an ancient lady. When his parents had disappeared one day when he was still too young to remember them, the elderly woman had appeared out of nowhere to care for him. She'd claimed to be his grandmother, but Chase hadn't recognized her. It didn't end up mattering because she'd raised him just the same.

Simone had done her best to curb his wanderings without damaging his boisterous and impulsive nature.

"Did you eat?" She grabbed her cane and limped toward the kitchen. "I could make oatmeal."

Chase grinned as he remembered the way he'd cajoled Deputy Dak into having breakfast. The big bear's rough demeanor had softened, fine sandpaper instead of coarse. "I ate. Can I fix you some oatmeal?"

"That would be lovely, dear, but you reek of things I'd rather not mention. Go take a shower." She patted his cheek and disappeared into the kitchen.

Heeding her advice, Chase headed down the hall, peeling out of his clothes as he made it to the bathroom. Simone was the one person to whom he didn't dare backtalk. She was sweet and kind, tiny and delicate—and he loved her more than anything in the world. He had no idea how old she was, and neither did anyone else. But when she told him to do something, he didn't argue.

An hour later, he sat at the table, drinking coffee with Simone.

"Are you going to work today?"

"I'm off today and tomorrow." Chase might like to party hard, but he never missed work.

She made an accepting sound. "I have errands to run."

"I'll take you."

Secure in the certainty his participation had never been in doubt, she patted his hand. "I want to have lunch at that café you took me to last week."

Chase searched his memory in an attempt to figure out which one she meant. While he took her out all the time, Simone's sense of time wasn't quite the same as his. He came up empty. "Which one is that?"

"The one with the apple pie."

Okay, not a café. That was a diner, and they'd eaten there six months ago. "Sure."

As they left, he wondered about the chances of running into that sexy deputy. Probably slim to none, and even if he did, Dak Freeman hadn't seemed interested in him.

Squiring Grandma around town exhausted Chase. She walked slowly, and she refused to use a wheelchair or a scooter. When selecting grocery and personal care items, she had to squint at the fine print on all the options before choosing the exact same product she always bought.

The entire ordeal was an exercise in patience and quelling his energetic nature for someone he loved. He didn't mind doing it—he even found contentment in it—but shopping for hours on end was tiring. He took a nap before heading out to The Bear's Den for another night of drinking and dancing.

He paid the cover and found Logan already on the dance floor surrounded by hard bodies. His buddy looked like happy meat in a sandwich, so Chase headed to the bar. He signaled for a beer.

"Hey, you're back." A hand landed on his hip, and a cock pressed into his ass cheek.

Chase turned his head to find Albert Houser, a predatory smile curving his lips. Ten years ago, he would have given anything to have Albert look at him that way, but right now, a pair of pale blue eyes danced in his vision. Shaking it away, he squeezed Albert's wrist. "Are you buying this round?"

"Sure." Albert signaled the bartender to put it on his tab. Then he wrapped his arm around Chase's waist and led him to a table. "I'm only back in town for a few days."

Chase didn't bother himself with gossip, so he hadn't known Albert had left. "Where are you going?"

"Back to the mountains. I've been living at the ranch, spending most of my time in bear form." He leaned closer and parked his hand on Chase's thigh. "It's freeing. You should come up with me."

They barely knew each other. To Chase's mind, they'd met that morning. The only things he remembered clearly from the night before involved time prior to Logan's bet and the moment Dak Freeman had shown up on the roof. He flashed a brief smile. "I like it here."

Albert chuckled as if he knew he was going to get his way eventually. "Want to get out of here?"

"I just got here."

"I know."

Rather than turn Albert down outright, Chase looked toward the dance floor. "Let's dance." Without waiting for a response, he downed his beer, grabbed Albert's hand, and dashed toward the crowd.

He pulled Albert through the sweaty crush of men until he found a small open spot. Albert moved his body, grinding it on a nearby ass to taunt Chase with the offer he hadn't accepted.

Not caring where Albert parked his dick, Chase threw himself into the party atmosphere. Several hours and many, many drinks later, Albert was once again at his elbow. He pulled Chase toward the front door. "C'mon. Let's get out of here."

Logan had left a while ago with a man Chase didn't know, so Chase followed Albert out of the club. The cooler air hit him, battling some of the queasiness that came from drinking one beer too many. Okay, he'd lost count of the number of drinks he'd downed.

At the corner, Albert pulled Chase into the dark alley between The Bear's Den and the restaurant next door. He pushed him against the brick, and before Chase knew what was happening, Albert's mouth was on his. Mind reeling and clouded by alcohol, Chase didn't protest.

He kissed Albert back. In the dark alley, they made out. Chase gripped Albert's shoulders. Though he had broader shoulders and larger muscles than Chase, Albert was short, which meant he had to rise to his tiptoes to kiss Chase the way he wanted.

Albert ground his cock against Chase's thigh and reached down Chase's jeans. In seconds, he pulled away, sputtering. "You're not even halfway hard."

Chase shrugged. "I drank a lot."

"Give me a blowjob." Something dangerous glittered behind Albert's eyes. "I paid your bar tab, party boy."

It hadn't bothered Chase when Deputy Dak had called him that, but the sneer in Albert's tone didn't sit right with him, and he realized his companion had not been drinking. He shoved the shorter man away. "Go fuck yourself."

Albert, sober and strong, pushed back. On instinct, Chase shifted. His clothes tore from his body as he assumed his bear form. He grunted and snuffled, warning Albert to back off, but the other man laughed.

"Oh, my. Aren't you just the most adorable little brown bear I've ever seen. You're not much larger than a cub." Albert fell against the brick and clutched his stomach.

With a rumble, Chase rose to his hind legs and pinned the fucking clown to the brick. He bared his teeth.

Albert's laughter turned into shrieks. The next thing Chase knew, a million volts were running through him, and the world went dark.

He woke up on the floor of a jail cell, naked and cold. Gingerly he climbed onto the bunk in the corner and covered himself with the thin blanket that reeked of chemicals.

On the other side of the bars was a single desk and chair positioned so the guard could cover the door and still see the prisoners in either cell.

This wasn't the first time Chase had awoken in jail—drunken brawls littered his nights—but it was the first time he'd been naked.

The door opened, and a guard entered. No—not a guard. It was Dak Freeman.

Chase pasted on his best flirty grin and ignored the pounding in his skull. "Hey, Deputy Dak. Is it your turn to buy me breakfast?"

A hint of a frown was Dak's only response. He left, and when he returned ten minutes later, he had a small tray. He slid it through the horizontal slat in the cell door.

With rubbery legs, Chase made the trek of three steps to collect the tray. The blanket fell off, but he didn't care. Let the deputy see what he was missing out on.

Except Dak's gaze didn't lower. He directed his emotionless stare to Chase's forehead.

Chase batted his eyelashes. "Was it something I said?"

For a second, Dak's gaze met Chase's. The electricity that had jolted through him the night before had nothing on the sparks igniting now.

Only Dak didn't seem to notice. His mouth tightened. "Do you have anyone to call who can post bail?"

"Bail?" He wolfed down the contents of the tiny plastic bowl of cereal. "Why do I need bail? Are you charging me with drunk and disorderly?"

Dak parked himself at the desk and opened a file folder. "You might want to think about an alcohol rehab program."

"I'm not an alcoholic." He knocked back the cold, bitter coffee in the paper cup. This was a far cry from the breakfast he'd offered Dak the morning before.

Dak grunted his disagreement.

"Fuck you." Chase picked up the blanket and wrapped it around his waist. "You don't know me."

"I know your type."

"No, you don't." The pout he affected was real, not the flirty attempt it had been the last time he'd stuck his lip out around Officer Sexy.

"I'm not arguing with you. Do you have someone I can call or not?"

Chase shrugged. Under no circumstances was he going to call Simone. It would break her heart to know he'd been arrested. Logan might come through. He rattled off his best friend's name and number.

Dak wrote it down, and then he left the lockup area.

Time passed—an hour, then two. Chase seethed as he watched the minute hand wend around the face of the clock hanging over the guard's desk. Sometimes Logan was an asshole. He was wealthy, from the right part of town, and his parents frowned on the idea of him hanging out with Chase. Even in school, their friendship had consisted of clandestine meetings.

Where Logan had a lot of friends, Chase had a lot of acquaintances.

Five hours passed before Dak returned. By that time, Chase had shifted into a bear—it was a lot warmer—and he prowled the cage. Anger rolled from him, reflected off the cinderblock walls, and battered back into his ursine form.

Dak stood on the other side of the bars, unimpressed. "Albert Houser decided not to press charges for the way you threatened and attacked him last night."

The reasons he'd shifted last night came back to him. Albert had ordered Chase to give him head because he'd paid the bar tab, and then he'd mocked Chase in his bear form. Chase transformed into his human form, wrapped the blanket around his hips, and gripped the bars. "That fucker comes near me, and I'll rip his fucking head off."

Impassive as ever, Dak didn't react except to cross his arms. A warning blazed in his mesmerizing blue eyes. "Are you honestly threatening to harm someone in front of an officer of the law?"

Humiliation rose in Chase's throat, bitter bile that had him swallowing down the emotion. He turned away from the handsome, disapproving deputy.

The door squeaked as it opened, the edge scraping across the cement floor. Dak wound a hand around Chase's arm and jerked him back so they were face-to-face. Dak's hot breath fanned Chase's face, and danger blazed from his eyes. "Answer me, cub."

Fascinated by the larger man's display of temper and how the fire it engendered in his belly eclipsed the humiliation he'd felt moments before, Chase smiled. "He pulls the same shit he pulled last night, and yeah, I'll react the same way."

Dak pressed his lips together. "What shit did he pull?"

Unwilling to go into specifics, Chase glanced away. "Am I getting out of here or what?"

"As far as I'm concerned, you can sit here until you learn how to answer a simple question." Dak released him suddenly and paced away, putting distance between them.

How dare he abuse his power to keep Chase imprisoned when he should be setting him free? In an impulsive fit of fury, Chase picked up the flimsy plastic bowl from breakfast and flung it at Dak's head.

It hit, the soft impact barely making a sound. The empty bowl was the equivalent of throwing a hand towel.

Still, Chase knew he'd fucked up even before Dak turned back to him. He shrunk away and lifted a hand to ward off whatever was coming his way. Nobody was around. Dak could beat the shit out of him, and nobody would believe Chase hadn't started it, not with his record.

Dak seized the wrist of the hand Chase held up, and jerked the smaller man forward. He ripped the blanket away, exposing Chase's body, and yet Chase wasn't afraid that the deputy might sexually assault him.

"You need to learn manners, cub." With that, Dak lifted Chase.

When he came down, Chase found himself across Dak's lap. The larger man had thrown a leg over Chase's legs, pinning them down. One hand between his shoulder blades held his torso in place.

The position made him feel helpless and curiously safe. Chase's mind rebelled even as his body softened into acceptance. "You can't spank me."

"You attacked me. It's this, or I write up the incident and you find yourself behind bars for the next thirty days. Your choice."

Thirty days meant Chase would lose his job. Though he was a damned good mechanic, he was replaceable. Right now, he hated Dak Freeman. "Fine." He forced his body to relax.

The first few smacks were too light to register as anything significant, and so Chase actually relaxed. After a time, Dak paused. "That was the warmup. Now we'll get serious. Twenty should do it. Count them out."

The next one seared his ass. Chase cried out and bucked. Thankfully Dak had a solid hold on him, so he didn't fall off the bed.

"They only count if you do." Dax landed another firm spank.

"Two," Chase yelped.

"One," Dak corrected. "No skipping numbers."

At five, Chase's ass cheeks burned. At ten, they were on fire. By the time fifteen rolled around, the pain had morphed into a curiously delicious sensation. Yes, his rear end hurt, but his cock was waking up. Each smack rubbed it against Dak's pant leg, and Chase became aware that his hip was nestled against the deputy's crotch.

There was no way Dak wasn't aware with each and every blow rocking Chase's body forward and back.

And anyone within hearing distance knew the moment Chase's cries changed from protests to begging.

Chapter Four

Dak rubbed his palm over Chase's reddened posterior. The miscreant wouldn't sit comfortably for several hours, after which all evidence would fade.

The cub draped over his lap made no move to get up even though the punishment had concluded. In fact, evidence he'd eventually enjoyed it pressed against Dak's thigh.

He eased Chase off his lap, acutely aware he'd crossed a line that could end his career. Chase lumbered to his feet and stared at Dak. All the attitude he'd carried before seemed to have vanished, and he regarded Dak with wide eyes and a hint of awe.

"Nobody's ever spanked me before."

"That explains a lot." Dak handed Chase the blanket and watched while he wrapped it around his hips.

"I'm not a drunk," he repeated, though the defensiveness and anger in his tone had vanished. "I go to the club on the nights I don't have to work the next day."

With Chase's second appearance in his life, Dak had looked up Chase's file. "You have six arrests for public drunkenness and brawling."

Chase shrugged and glanced away. "I'm sure you're not interested in the circumstances."

"Nope." Dak had figured out Chase was mostly bluster, and his knack for finding trouble led to most of his problems.

Gesturing to the open cell door, Chase said, "Am I free to go?"

Dak's gaze roamed down the expanse of naked chest to the blanket tucked like a skirt around Chase's waist. That man was far too handsome for his own good. "Do you want pants?"

"Sure." He pursed his lips. "You wouldn't happen to know where my keys and wallet are?"

Dak had collected the torn clothing from the ground in the alley. "All your stuff is bagged and locked up. I'll get it for you." He motioned for Chase to follow him, and he headed to the cell door.

The lost and found had a pair of sweats that were tight and short on Chase, but once he slid them over his slim hips, Dak couldn't find fault with the look. He'd already prepared the paperwork, so Chase only had to sign, and then he could go.

He scrawled his signature.

"You're free."

19

"Am I?"

Dak glanced up from stamping the signature to find Chase regarding him with devilry sparkling in his eyes. Before he could reply, the smaller man's lips pressed to his. Dak was the kind of man who had to be in charge, and so before his brain could scream at him that he was courting ten kinds of trouble, he grasped Chase's neck, tilting his head back to deepen the kiss.

Chase's lips were soft and inviting, everything a cub should be. For the past couple days, Dak had been using 'cub' to indicate Dak was acting younger than his age. But right now, it took on a whole new meaning, one that caused Dak's cock to wake up and demand attention.

Finally his sense of self-preservation kicked in, and Dak ended the kiss before it could become anything more.

Chase stepped back, breathing hard, and that impish smile brightened his face. "Damn, that was hot. Thank you—for everything. I can't remember the last time I enjoyed being locked up quite so much."

As Chase left, Dak realized that the cub had thanked him for the spanking as well as the kiss. For the rest of the day, nothing diminished the smile on Dak's face.

That evening, Evan Chillwell came in to relieve Dak from desk duty. A few years older than Dak, the friendly deputy had welcomed Dak with open arms, as had the entire staff in the Bear's Cove Sheriff's office.

"Quiet day, Freeman?" Evan set his hat on the desk and perched on the corner.

Dak glanced up from the crossword puzzle he'd been working on. A million thoughts raced through his mind. For the past three hours, he'd replayed the experience of spanking Chase's luscious ass, and he kept touching his lips as he remembered the kiss. "Fairly."

"I heard you arrested Chase Longfellow again last night."

"Yeah." That was a matter of public record. Many people had witnessed Chase shift into his bear form and threaten Albert. "Houser declined to press charges."

Evan lifted a brow. "I heard you had to taser him."

"Yeah." He hadn't liked hurting Chase that way, but the cub hadn't left him a choice. He'd called for Chase to stand down, but the bear had been too enraged to listen. "He spent the night sleeping it off."

Pacing to the window, Evan peered into a small parking lot that housed the squad cars and the personal vehicles of the officers, staff, and the firefighters in the building next door. "That boy sure got a raw deal."

Dak's ears perked up. Beating back the need to jump up and demand the full story, Dak opted for the casual approach. "Oh?"

"Yep. His parents disappeared under mysterious circumstances and were never found. It's a cold case. When I got here sixteen years ago, it was still hot, you know?"

A detail nagged at Dak. "There was nothing in Longfellow's file about it." He'd unearthed all the arrests, none of which had resulted in charges.

"He had a different name back then—Bacoel." Evan opened a cabinet and dug through the files. "Here it is." He set it on the desk in front of Dak. "This is not for the faint of heart."

Nothing had ever deterred Dak from pursuing the truth, and he had a desperate need to know more about the man who'd hijacked his thoughts. He tapped a finger on the unopened folder. "Why are you showing this to me?"

Settling into a nearby chair, Evan rested his feet on the desk next to the file. "Because you've got that look."

Having honed the art of hiding his emotions, Dak lifted his brows. "What look? One that says I want to solve cold cases?" He didn't mind going after cases nobody had been able to close. Bear's Cove had very little crime, so they definitely had enough time to pursue cold cases.

"You've picked up Chase Longfellow twice in two days." Evan threaded his hands together behind his neck as he got comfortable. "As long as no one gets hurt, we don't arrest him. All the arrests you see in his file are newbies who didn't know to leave him alone."

That didn't sit right with Dak. No matter what happened in Chase's past, he shouldn't get a free pass to go around misbehaving. "He threw bottles off the roof of The Bear's Den, and then last night, he threatened Albert Houser."

Evan waved a hand, dismissing Dak's concern. "Houser had it coming. That little shit needs his fathers to take him in hand. Longfellow blows off steam on the weekends. Let him go. It's all he has."

"You're saying I should ignore the calls?"

"No. I'm saying you handle the calls. Take him home. His grandmother, Simone Longfellow, will set him to rights. She has a special way with him." Evan flashed a brief smile. "Open the file folder. You'll see what I mean."

Curiosity got the better of Dak. He opened the file to see a typed report. File photos paper-clipped to the top showed a handsome man and a beautiful woman. The woman had Chase's laughing eyes, and the man had his floppy blond hair and pointed chin.

His gaze scanned the report. Two deputies had responded to a late night call complaining of a noisy neighbor. They found a house full of blood and fur, but no bodies. In the back bedroom, they found a boy asleep in the closet under a mound of clothes and blankets. Rather than take him through the gruesome scene, they rescued him through the window, telling him that there was a fire.

The next morning, Simone Longfellow showed up at the station to claim her grandson. Though he'd followed simple commands and responded to stimuli, the boy hadn't spoken a single word all night. Deputies speculated about what he knew or might have heard. Surely he'd heard something because he'd stayed hidden in his room. Psychologists and other professionals had tried to talk to him about it, but he'd clammed up each time.

Next Dak looked at the crime scene photographs. Blood splattered the walls and saturated the carpet. Tufts of fur and skin were found all over the place. Nobody could have survived losing that much blood, yet the bodies were never found.

Dak closed the file and set it aside. Silence reigned for several pensive minutes. Finally he cleared his throat. "This doesn't explain why he should be given a free pass to wreak havoc on the town."

"Freeman, we like you. We'll stick by you. But leave the kid alone."

To Dak's way of thinking, Chase was a twenty-three-year-old man, not a kid. And he'd responded to a spanking by calming down and thanking Dak. No, the town was wrong to pussyfoot around Chase. Dak stood and grabbed his keys. "I'm going to call it a day. I promise not to arrest him tonight as long as he doesn't do anything illegal in front of me."

That night as he grilled a steak, images from the file kept flashing through Dak's mind. The crime scene seemed so haphazard. Nothing made sense, not the splatter patterns or the location of the fur. It was a conundrum for sure, and with no witnesses except a six-year-old child, it wasn't surprising nobody had been able to solve it.

Sometime after dinner, the phone rang, and he picked up on the first ring. "Cord. How are you, man?"

His friend's smile came right through the phone. "Great. You survived your first weekend in Bear's Cove. How do you think it went?"

Dak wondered if Cord was calling as a friend or as his boss. Rather than beat around the bush, he called him out. "Are you asking as my friend or as my superior?"

"Friend." Cord didn't hesitate. "You've been through a lot recently. I hope you're settling in."

Dak twisted the cap off a beer and flopped onto the sofa. "I'm settling in. Boxes are unpacked and put away. I broke in the new grill with a fantastic steak, and I'm about to watch some TV."

"You could come over," Cord offered. "Brock and I were going to binge-watch that new horror series."

Not that he'd ever admit it to anyone, but Dak hated horror movies. He could sink his teeth into a cop show or a love story, but not horror. "That's okay. I have eight episodes of North Woods Law waiting for me."

Cord was quiet for a moment. From the way the background noise muffled, Dak figured Cord had closed a door for privacy. "Evan said he talked to you."

"Yeah."

"Good." Cord exhaled a long stream of breath. "So you understand."

Dak pressed his lips together. "I'm still struggling with that. Nobody should get to flout the law. It's not right."

Rather than argue, Cord made a knowing sound. "I respect your perspective, and I'm glad you're enjoying Bear's Cove. Brock's calling me, so I'm going to get going. I'll see you tomorrow."

This was the second time in one day he'd been warned about cutting Chase some slack, and his gut told him Chase needed a firm hand more than a fifty-third chance.

The next day, Dak drove the patrol car around town, visiting people and getting to know them. At the end of his shift, he headed back to the small building housing their post.

Cord stood at the front desk, talking to a woman holding a basket of sausage.

Dak's nose twitched at the spicy aroma, and he peered at the basket.

She turned when he came in, a huge smile on her face. Dak noted she was around his age and in healthy physical condition. Her long hair was tied back in a ponytail, which made him happy because if she'd made the sausages, then it was imperative she keep her hair out of the mix.

She stuck out a hand. "Hi. I'm Mya Chillwell, Evan's sister. He said there was a new deputy in town."

Tearing his attention away from the fresh meat, he shook Mya's hand. "It's nice to meet you, Mya." He couldn't keep his gaze from wandering to the basket.

With a giggle, she shoved it at him. "I know your type, so I know exactly what you want. These are for you. Welcome to Bear's Cove."

"Mya is a butcher," Cord added. "She has a shop two streets over."

He accepted the basket. "This smells really good. Thank you."

"I was telling Cord we need to have a welcome dinner for you, get you introduced to everyone." She smiled, an expression that seemed to emanate from every pore. "I have to get going, but if you need meat, come see me. Special rate for law enforcement." Throwing a wink at Dak, she squeezed his arm and left.

Basket on his arm, Dak watched the woman exit.

"She's not into you," Cord said. "She's married and has three kids. She's just really nice."

Relieved he wouldn't have to fend off Evan's sister or feel guilty while devouring the basket full of different kinds of sausage, Dak nodded. "I was going to file my paperwork and head out for the day, unless you need me."

Cord scratched the back of his neck. "Submitting your log should only take a minute. The patrol car you were driving today is due for an inspection and oil change. Can you drop it at Fordline's Garage? They'll give you a ride back here."

"Yeah, sure." Ten minutes later, he pulled into the parking lot at Fordline's Garage. Nobody was at the front desk, so he headed into the garage in search of a body.

He found one bent over an open hood, his dark green coveralls clinging to a very familiar ass. This was unexpected. Dak took a moment to collect himself, which was difficult because looking at Chase's fine backside stirred a firestorm of lust.

"I know you're staring at my ass."

Dak started. Bears had a great sense of smell, but the scent of oil and grease permeating the shop had to override what he was giving off. Or maybe Chase was just being cocky. Dak exhaled, getting his libido under control. "Are you going to be long?"

Chase slowly unbent and turned around. His brilliant smile lit the space between them. "Deputy Freeman, did you come to arrest me again?"

Not willing to give this cub the upper hand, Dak came closer. "Listen, little cub, I don't give a flying fuck what kind of arrangement you have with the rest of the Sheriff's Department, but I don't feel sorry for you, and I'm not going to let you run around town acting like a delinquent."

Chase lifted a brow, but he didn't appear overly impressed. "Are we talking being arrested, or will I get handcuffed and spanked?" He wiped his hands on a towel that draped from his pocket, a cocky grin permanently etched on his face.

Not sure of how to answer, Dak remained impassive. When all else failed, his stoic stare had never let him down.

With a carefree laugh, Chase eliminated all but a few inches between them. "When you came in, I felt you looking at me. Did you enjoy the view?" He drew a finger down Dak's chest, circling the buttons on his brown shirt.

Dak seized Chase's hand, halting his foray. "Cub, you're playing with fire."

That cocky smile only grew. "Burn me, Daddy."

"I'm not flirting with you." He had to get the upper hand because Chase was damned cute and nearly irresistible. And calling him 'Daddy?' That was so fucking hot.

Chase's smile faded, and it was like the sun had disappeared behind a dark cloud. "That's unfortunate." He disengaged his hand from Dak's hold and turned away. "How can I help you, Deputy?"

"Patrol car needs an inspection and oil change."

Nodding, Chase disappeared through the door leading to the front desk. He returned a minute later and handed over a set of keys. "Take the loaner. I'll bring the patrol car to the station in a couple hours, and I'll pick up the loaner."

"I'm headed home." Cord had assured him that he'd get a ride back to the station, but Dak didn't see how Chase could leave. He was the only one there.

Chase lifted his shoulder. "I remember where you live. I'll bring it by when I'm finished."

Now Dak felt like a jerk. He had enjoyed Chase's flirting. In fact, he'd been thrilled by the cub's enthusiastic greeting. He absolutely hated how the inner joy had dimmed from Chase's eyes. "I don't want you to go out of your way."

Again, Chase lifted his shoulder as if it meant nothing to him. "No big deal. It's part of the job. We have a standing agreement with the Sheriff's office, so there's no paperwork you need to fill out or sign."

With that, Chase dismissed Dak's presence. He went back to the car he'd been working on when Dak arrived.

Feeling out of place, Dak found the loaner car and went home. After puttering around for an hour doing nothing, he decided to make dinner.

He started the rice steamer and threw salmon on the grill. It was far too much for one person, so it looked like he'd be having leftovers for a few days. Long enough to get sick of fish and not eat it for a year.

Didn't matter—he was unaccountably nervous, and he didn't have much of an appetite.

He changed three times. First he put on old sweats, and then he reasoned Chase would be swinging by soon. He didn't want to be wearing ratty clothes, not for company, even if he wasn't technically company. Then he changed to jeans that made his ass look really good, but then he figured Chase would know he was trying to impress him. Torn between limited options, Dak ended up wearing an older pair of jeans. These had rips on the legs, but they still emphasized his assets in an attractive way.

The shirt was much easier. He opted for a plain sky blue tee shirt because it brought out his eyes.

Then he wandered back into the kitchen to check the salmon.

"This is stupid," he muttered as he brushed a teriyaki mixture over the fish. "He's not coming for dinner. He's dropping off a fucking car, and you were a dick to him when he flirted, so he has no reason to think you even like him."

In the midst of his reverse pep talk, the doorbell rang. He closed the oven and rushed to the door, happy to see Chase even if it was just for a minute.

He opened the door to find a different Chase from the one he'd seen at the garage and the one he'd arrested twice. Wearing long cargo shorts and a white, short-sleeved button down shirt, he looked ready for a date. The shirt was casually untucked, and the top three buttons were undone. His hair had been styled to stay back from his face instead of falling over his eyes.

Chase had showered and changed before coming over.

Dak couldn't stop a small, triumphant grin from twisting his lips. He opened the door wider. "Come on in."

Chapter Five

Nerves randomly fired in Chase's body, making him feel off-kilter as he entered Dak's house. He should have come straight here from work. Beneath his greasy mechanic's coveralls, his clothes had been in fine shape. Except they smelled like the garage, and Dak had seemed strangely distant when he'd come by.

Dak's fingertips were a gentle pressure on Chase's lower back. "Are you hungry?"

This wasn't a date. No matter what kind of mixed signals he was getting from Dak, the last one had been clear—he wasn't flirting. Of course, Dak hadn't flirted at all. In flashes and moments, there had been hints of desire, the chemical pull of attraction, and that spanking. The skin on Chase's ass heated just from the memory.

This wasn't a date—except Dak had changed into jeans that made the bulge at the apex of his thighs look that much larger and a shirt that emphasized his wide shoulders and strong chest. The short sleeves strained to cover Dak's massive biceps.

Chase leaned into the hand on his back, turning to face Dak. Inches separated them. He held up the key to the patrol car. "I brought these."

Dak's clear blue gaze didn't acknowledge the statement. Wordlessly he demanded a response.

"I'm hungry." He didn't specify exactly what he was craving. Though whatever was in the oven smelled scrumptious, Chase wanted to taste something else. Right now, he wanted another kiss from the deputy. Not one to wait for what he wanted, Chase rose to his toes and pressed his lips to Dak's. It was an offering, and his heart pounded so hard he thought it might burst out of his chest.

Dak's fingertips slid to Chase's waist, the pressure increasing until his grip was firm. Dak's tongue traced along Chase's lower lip, and Chase opened to this gentle request.

Once he did that, all bets were off. Dak gripped the back of Chase's neck, tilting his head to let Dak's tongue inside. With his kiss, he ravaged Chase's mouth and liquefied his bones. Chase sagged against Dak, trusting the stronger man to take his weight. While Chase had an average build, standing next to Dak, he felt almost tiny.

Dak banded an arm around Chase's waist, molding their bodies together. He broke the kiss to trail sucking bites along Chase's jaw and down his neck. With a smile, Chase congratulated himself on having stopped home to shower and shave.

Chase moaned. "Oh, Daddy, that feels really good."

Dak planted one last kiss at the base of Chase's throat, and then he eased back. "Why do you keep calling me that?"

"What? Daddy?"

"Yeah. I'm not your father."

"Ewww." Chase pushed playfully against Dak's chest, and his would-be lover didn't move an inch. "Not like that. You're an alpha, in charge. The boss. You spanked me—like a Daddy bear."

He watched as Dak digested his explanation. Chase knew the image of him in Dak's eyes was tarnished at best. Or perhaps this alpha was too young to have embraced his true nature? Though it went against his natural impulsivity, Chase forced himself to wait for Dak's response.

A million thoughts went through Dak's eyes, like the scroll at the bottom of the TV screen on the news programs his grandma liked to watch. Like those words, Chase didn't bother trying to read them. But with Dak, he cared about the meaning and the implications.

After a time, Dak nodded. "We're going to have dinner."

"It smells delicious." Knowing things were decided in his favor, Chase grinned.

"We'll talk. Other than your record, I know very little about you."

To this, Chase shrugged. "There's not much to tell. My parents died when I was too young to remember them. I was raised by my grandma, who I love more than anything in this world, and the rest, you know."

Dak pressed a fingertip to Chase's lips, stilling the flow of words. "If dinner goes well, we'll talk about what we want to happen tonight."

Chase knew what he wanted to happen tonight, and dinner was just foreplay. But he also knew when he wasn't in charge, so he put himself in Dak's capable hands.

"Dinner is almost ready."

Chase followed Dak to the kitchen. The small condo was in a row of single-story homes in a newer subdivision on the edge of the city. It wasn't larger than the home where he'd grown up, but it was newer, and it was on the right side of the tracks. Where Chase lived, the homes were much older and often in need of expensive repairs.

When he'd woken up in the living room only a few mornings ago, Chase had noted the simple layout—kitchen behind the living room, bathroom and bedroom off to the side. He hadn't been in the bedroom—yet.

The modern kitchen had a sleek look with stark whites, stainless steel appliances, and white plastic cabinets. It was all very stylish, and a bit cold.

"Sit." Dak pointed to the small table to one side of the kitchen. "I'll get the food."

"I don't mind helping." Chase set a hand on Dak's arm. "I know my way around a kitchen."

Dak's blue eyes lightened. "You can set the table."

Wasting no time, Chase set to work. He opened a cupboard he thought would contain plates, and he clapped to find he was right. "What do you have to drink?"

Dak's finger morphed to a bear claw, and he sliced open the foil on the salmon. "Water for you, cub. I'd like to see if your claim of not being an alcoholic is true."

Even though wine would be more romantic and Chase had spied a wine rack, he let the idea slide away. From Dak's perspective, Chase did look like the town drunk. "Do you have any lemon juice?"

"In the fridge."

Chase added a squirt of lemon juice to the water to freshen up the flavor. He liked flavor in his beverages. "So, what do you want to know about me?"

As he scooped rice from the steamer into a serving bowl, Dak pursed his lips. "What made you decide to become a mechanic?"

"I'm good with my hands." Chase's lips curved, and he shot a sultry look in Dak's direction. "As you're about to find out."

Dak set the bowl of rice and the plate with salmon in the center of the table Chase had set. His lips pressed together briefly, and he didn't respond to Chase's look. He pulled out Chase's chair and gestured for him to sit. "For real, Chase. Why did you decide to become a mechanic?"

Dropping his flirty demeanor, Chase shrugged. "I started tinkering with things when I was little. We had a toaster that didn't work. I took it apart and replaced the heating coil. After that, I moved on to other small appliances. In high school, I took auto shop classes, and then I started working at Fordline's."

"Why not open your own shop?"

Chase wrinkled his nose as he heaped rice on his plate. "Why? Fordline's was already there, and I like fixing things, not running a business."

"What appeals to you about being a mechanic?" Dak cut the salmon in quarters and set a hefty steak on top of Chase's pile of rice.

"I already said I like fixing things." Chase laughed. "Are you nervous, Dak? Has it been a while since your last date?"

Dak's eyes flared. "I meant most people choose a profession based on what they find fulfilling. When I saw you in the garage, for the first time since we've met, you looked comfortable and confident."

The comment rubbed Chase the wrong way. "I'm generally confident."

"You're generally cocky." Dak sipped the water, his eyebrow rising slightly. "This is good with lemon."

"I know."

Half-grinning, Dak said, "That's it, right there. You're cocky, which is often a sign of false confidence. You use it to disguise vulnerability."

Nobody had ever noticed that about Chase before. Shifting uncomfortably, he stuck a fork into the salmon, tearing off a large chunk. "I'm good-looking, young, and gifted with my hands. I have no reason not to be confident. I'm not disguising anything. What you see is what you get."

Dak watched him while he chewed. Then he swallowed and licked his lips, reminding Chase of how they felt on his. "I see a man who drinks to excess every week, which leads him to make other poor decisions. If you weren't hiding anything, you wouldn't feel the need to soak your brain in alcohol."

People didn't speak to Chase this way. Not since he was a little boy had anyone tried to press him about why he did the things he did. He didn't have answers now anymore than he had then. Scowling, he stabbed his fork into the salmon and left it there, and he lashed out. "Do you psychoanalyze every man before you fuck them?"

"Just the ones who interest me." Dak didn't seem ruffled by Chase's display of temper. "I find you fascinating, Chase Longfellow. You told me there was more to you, and you were right. I'm trying to figure out which is your true face."

Chase resumed eating. "I'm not as complex as you're making me seem. I'm a late-blooming bear shifter who is still enjoying his juvenile phase. I like to have fun, Dak. That's what I was hoping for when I came here tonight—fun."

Shades of sadness flickered through Dak's eyes, but they were gone, replaced by calm acceptance so quickly that Chase doubted what he'd seen. Dak watched Chase eat, so Chase slowed down, exaggerating his movements to make the simple act of putting food in his mouth sensual.

Dak seemed mesmerized, which suited Chase just fine.

"What made you decide to become a deputy?" Chase strove for a casual tone. "Did your love of handcuffs come before or after your career choice?"

Dak's smile turned downright predatory. "Before."

"Are you going to tie me up, Deputy Freeman?"

"Would you like to be tied up, Chase?"

Chase thought about that one, but he couldn't arrive at a conclusion. "I don't know. I've never done it before. I'm eager to find out, though. You could spank me again, if you wanted."

Dak's clear blue gaze turned to molten steel, but he steered the topic back to neutral waters. "My fathers were cops. I grew up wanting to be just like them, but they wanted me to be a lawyer. I got a law degree, and I worked in a law office for a few years. My heart wasn't in it, so here I am."

"So simple." Chase used his teasing grin this time. Dak was proving impossible to manipulate, and Chase was finding he liked not being able to get the upper hand. "See? Most people's motivations are obvious."

Dak finished his meal, propped his elbows on the table, and folded his hands. "I'll spank you, cub, but you'll have to earn it."

A shiver traveled to Chase's cock. "I will, Daddy."

"I'm going to put away the leftovers."

Chase leaped up. "I'll clear the table." Without waiting for Dak to respond, he scraped and rinsed dishes, and he loaded them into the dishwasher. His grandma had trained him to always do his part, and he wouldn't feel right if he didn't.

When he went for the pan, Dak's hand closed over his. "Leave it." He trapped Chase between his body and the counter, pressing his front against Chase's.

Chase reached to his sides and gripped the edge of the counter as Dak's mouth closed over his. This kiss was different from the others. It contained a hunger and a certainty that had been absent before, and Chase felt his body responding to these new demands.

With a rumbled moan deep in his chest, Chase released his grip on the countertop. He slid his hands up Dak's chest, exploring that vast expanse with a firm pressure. The larger man groaned and broke off the endless, searing kiss.

"Bedroom," he said.

It wasn't far. Chase held Dak's hand and followed him obediently. The shades were drawn, so even though the sun hadn't set, the room was cast in shadows. Dak hit the light switch, and Chase smiled. He had sex in the dark most of the time because quick, one-night stands

31

happened in alleys or in dark corners of a bar. He wanted this to be different.

The room was twice as large as the one Chase had at home. It had all the regular bedroom furniture, but the best part was the king-sized bed dominating the space.

Dak's arms came around Chase's waist, and he ground his cock against Chase's ass. Chase pressed back and moaned. "Oh, Daddy. I can't wait to feel you inside me."

"I bite," Dak said.

Biting among their kind wasn't common in quick hookups. Chase shivered in Dak's arms. "Do you break the skin?"

"Sometimes, if you fight it."

So the choice was Chase's. If he wanted it to be violent and brutal, he could resist. "I won't."

Dak's large hand kneaded his ass through the thickness of Chase's cargo shorts. Then he reached around and undid the button and zipper in front. The shorts slid down Chase's legs, and Dak's hand slid under the waistband of Chase's underwear. "You're so fucking sexy, cub." He closed his hand around Chase's hard cock. "And big. Wow. You're huge."

Chase chuckled. "Yep. I'm fucking hot and well-hung. Now you see why I'm so cocky."

Dak's other hand gripped Chase's ball sac. Chase sucked in a breath at the pleasure rocketing through his system. Dak squeezed lightly, rolling the sac in his palm as his other hand worked the length of Chase's cock.

Like magnets, his hands sought Dak's body. He gripped the alpha's thighs. "I see you have talented hands as well."

Dak's laugh was decidedly sinister. "Call me 'Daddy.' I like it."

"Daddy, I love what your hands are doing to my massive cock." He meant to follow up with a flirty laugh, but he could only manage a moan.

Dak released his hold on Chase's cock and balls. His touch feathered upward, unbuttoning Chase's shirt as it went. In a series of kisses and deft touches, he undressed Chase and guided him to the bed.

Lost in a riot of sensation, Chase felt the edge of the mattress nudge the backs of his legs. He wrapped his arms around Dak's neck and pulled his lover down on top of him. They tumbled, a mass of groping arms and legs, wrestling until they were both naked.

32

Chase gripped Dak's cock, gasping when he couldn't quite wrap his entire hand around the thick member. "My, Daddy, what a chubby cock you have. I'm definitely going to feel this. If I'm lucky—for days."

Dak ripped his lips and body away suddenly, springing to his feet and pacing the length of the bed.

Lost in the moment, shock took a moment to register in Chase's brain. "Dak? What's wrong?"

"Nothing's wrong. I want you so fucking bad, if I don't back off, I'm going to come on you instead of in you."

Reassured that nothing was wrong, Chase sprawled on his back and stroked his cock. "We've got all night. Fuck me fast, and we can take our time later."

Dak wrapped a hand around his cock and crooked a finger at Chase. "Come sit on the edge of the bed."

Wearing his best pout, Chase slid to the edge nearest his lover. "Are you going to fuck my mouth, Daddy?"

"Yes."

Chase wet his lips and let saliva pool around his tongue.

Dak traced the crown of his penis on Chase's lips, and Chase's tongue darted out for a taste. Dak threaded his fingers through Chase's hair and tugged. "Cub, how much can you take?"

He knew what his alpha wanted to know, and now wasn't the time for boasting. Using both hands, Chase measured the length and thickness of Dak's cock. While it was a good length, it was the circumference that posed the largest concern. He giggled. "I can't unhinge my jaw, so if you can get it in, I can take it all."

Dak stroked Chase's cheek. "This will get rough."

A thrill ran through Chase's body, and heat rose in his cheeks at how much he craved Dak's firm and unrelenting hand. Feeling desired like this boosted Chase's cheekiness. He licked the underside of Dak's cock. "Don't worry—I don't bite."

With a husky chuckle, Dak slipped the tip of his cock into Chase's mouth. "That's a good cub. Get it nice and wet. Now, no more touching your cock. Show me how good you are with your hands while I fuck this luscious mouth."

Chase hollowed out his cheeks and sucked harder. He wrapped one hand around the base of Dak's cock, and he fondled Dak's balls with the other.

Soft sounds of pleasure poured from his alpha. Taking his time, Chase used his tongue to find the places and pressures that made Dak gasp the loudest.

Soon both of Dak's hands grasped Chase's head. Playtime was over. Chase inhaled through his nose and relaxed his jaw as Dak pushed in farther. The tip of his cock nudged the back of Chase's throat, and he swallowed.

"Fuck, Chase, you feel amazing." Dak's forward momentum stopped. "That's all of it. You're choking on my cock like a good cub."

The praise went a long way toward helping Chase accept the strain of serving his Daddy. Pain prickled the back of his throat, and tears burned his eyes.

Dak eased all the way out, a string of saliva the only thing linking them together. "Breathe when I pull out, my handsome cub. This won't take long."

"Yes, Daddy."

"You'll swallow it all."

"Oh, yes, Daddy."

With that, Dak surged forward. This foray wasn't gentle. He held Chase's head still as he fucked his mouth. Low growls sounded in the back of his throat, vibrations designed to drive Dak's pleasure even higher.

Chase submitted to Dak's demands, becoming a vessel for his pleasure. He released the base of Dak's cock to trail a finger along his alpha's taint. Knowing Dak was close, Chase eased a finger into Dak's anus and massaged his prostate.

"Oh, fuck, yeah." Dak surged forward, burying his cock so deep it crushed Chase's lips against his teeth.

Hot jets of semen spurted down Chase's throat, and he swallowed it all.

Dak eased his cock out, and then he flopped onto the bed. "Give me a minute, cub." He rolled to his side. "Stroke your cock, but don't come."

Chase snuggled his head against Dak's shoulder and pressed his side to his alpha's warm body. While he waited for Dak to recover, he lazily masturbated.

Dak slid his arm under Chase to hold him closer, and his fingers played up and down Chase's back. "I'm going to spank you, my precious cub, just like you asked for. Do you want me to use my hand or a belt?"

The question shocked Chase. "I don't know. I liked what you did to me before. That's my only experience with spanking."

His alpha pressed a kiss to his forehead. "Trust me?"

The funny thing about trust was how much was expected and how little was actually given. In his entire life, Chase had trusted very few people. Logan was his best friend, but Chase only trusted him so far. His grandma was the only person who'd never broken his trust.

Dak only asked for a little bit, and so Chase decided to give it to him. "Okay."

Hugging him closer, Dak tilted Chase's face up. His mouth closed over Chase's, capturing and claiming in one deft move. Chase melted, his body conforming to Dak's contours and his heart joining the fray.

"I want you to kneel facing the headboard. Grip the top rail." Dak helped position Chase toward the left side of the bed with his knees spread, running his hands over Chase's body until the cub was completely relaxed. "This is for pleasure, not punishment, so no counting. Just enjoy it, cub. I'm going to make you come."

Chase wasn't sure a spanking could make him come, but it felt good, and that was enough for now.

As if sensing his thoughts, Dak bent down and closed his mouth around Chase's cock. Chase hissed with pleasure as Dak sucked it in. As Chase's cock was longer and the angle was bad, he didn't expect his alpha to deep-throat him, but what he was doing felt so fucking wonderful.

After a few moments, Dak released his cock with a loud, smacking kiss. "Face the headboard, cub, and don't move."

"Yes, Daddy."

Dak's weight left the bed, and Chase heard him moving around in the room. He fought the temptation to cave to curiosity. Sounds happened—a drawer opening and closing, items added to the nightstand. It seemed like a lot of time passed, but only a few minutes had elapsed.

Dak's lips pressed to Chase's shoulder, startling him. "You were good." He wrapped a hand around Chase's cock and pumped it while his mouth claimed Chase's once again.

Chase found that he loved Dak's kisses. They were wet and hot, comforting and passionate at the same time. For the first time, Chase wanted to lay in bed with a man, snuggling and kissing.

The kiss ended, and Dak moved away. He felt the heat and gentle pressure of Dak's touch on his ass and thighs. "If you need it lighter or harder, ask for it, okay? I'm learning what you like, and that means I need you to be honest and vocal."

"Yes, Daddy."

The first smack landed. It was light in comparison to what Dak had leveled on him in the jail cell. Chase didn't jump, twitch, or try to pull away. It hadn't hurt at all. In fact, it had felt damned good. Dak hit again and again. The smacks came faster and harder, building in heat and intensity.

Chase's cock throbbed. He desperately wanted to masturbate, but he knew Dak didn't want him to come just yet, so he gripped the top rail harder.

The spanking stopped. Dak trailed a fingertip over Chase's ass, sending shivers spiraling in all directions. His entire body shuddered. "How are you doing, sexy cub? Can you take more?"

Could he? "Yes. It doesn't hurt at all, Daddy. It feels so good."

"Are you close to coming?"

"I'm okay as long as you don't touch my dick."

Chase felt Dak's hot hand wrap around his sac. Ever so gently, he pulled down. Pleasure-pain too intense to process spiked through Chase's body. He cried out, a loud shout as a climax detonated in his core. Semen shot from his cock onto the slats and the wall behind the headboard.

His entire body trembling, Chase struggled to remain in place. Tears leaked from his eyes, a reaction to extreme and unexpected pleasure. "Fuck, Daddy. What did you do to me?"

Chapter Six

Dak pried Chase's fingers from the top rail. Trembling from head to toe, Chase curled into him as he lifted the cub and laid him on the bed. He stroked sweaty strands of hair away from Chase's face as he chuffed soothing sounds to his lover.

Once the trembling eased, Dak grabbed the wet wipes on the nightstand and washed ejaculate off the wall, chuckling softly as he recalled the shock that had registered on Chase's face when he'd come.

Never in his life had a lover responded to him the way Chase did. From their first meeting, Chase had been open and unabashedly honest. For all his party boy lifestyle, he had an innocence about him that called to Dak's alpha nature. This was new to Dak. He'd always known he preferred to be in charge, but he'd never met someone who needed him to take control the way Chase did. He settled his body next to Chase's so that his cub's head nestled in the crook of his arm, and pulled the sheet over their cooling bodies.

Chase's hands moved in a lazy pattern over Dak's chest. "I've never—I mean, I didn't know—"

Dak brought Chase's hand to his mouth and kissed his palm. "I know, my precious cub. I know. We'll rest up and do it again."

A half-hearted laugh erupted from Chase. "Damn. You know exactly what to say to set a guy's heart all aflutter."

"This is foreplay. I still haven't fucked you."

"Sweet talker. I am so lucky you broke with tradition and arrested me."

Dak tilted Chase's face up so he could see it. "You know about that?"

"That the deputies won't arrest me? Yeah. It's kind of obvious." Chase's gaze darted away. "I'm kind of tainted, so even they want to steer clear."

"Tainted?" Dak didn't like that word, and he hated the fact his cub had such a low opinion of himself. "Don't say that."

"It's true, Deputy Daddy." Chase rolled to his stomach, depriving Dak of half his body heat. The cub frowned, which was a cute expression on his handsome face, but the reason for it bothered Dak. "Didn't they tell you?"

Dak wasn't sure how much he wasn't supposed to say. "Evan told me on Sunday I was supposed to give you a warning and drive you home."

Chase snorted. "Not that. They feel sorry for me because my parents were murdered while I was asleep, and they never caught the murderers. Some people think it's eerie that I didn't wake up, like maybe I did it, or they think I'm bad luck—tainted. A lot of people avoid me or they avoid getting close to me. Even Logan, my best friend, keeps our relationship a secret from his parents. They would fire me if they knew."

Dak's stomach dropped. "That's horrible. Who the fuck would think a six-year-old could do that?"

A sly grin played on Chase's face. "So they did show you the file. I guess you're finished arresting me."

"Because you're finished doing dumb shit. No more drunk-and-disorderly. No more drinking until you pass out."

Chase shoved at his chest. "You tasered me. I didn't pass out."

"You shifted and threatened Albert Houser."

With a casual lift of his shoulder, Chase brushed off the accusation. "He had it coming."

Dak wanted to counter that nobody had it coming, but he wanted to know Chase's side, and admonishing him would only shut him down. "What did he do?"

The playful light in Chase's eyes dimmed, and he rolled away, resting his head on his own pillow. "Doesn't matter. I handled it. It's in the past."

Sensing they were close to a sensitive place, Dak refused to let his cub hide. In one swift move, he covered Chase's lithe body with his bulkier one. Pinning his cub in place to strip him of an escape—physical or emotional—Dak growled. "What did he do?"

Chase pushed against his shoulders, so he held the smaller man's wrists to the bed.

"Chase—I'll ask one more time. What did he do?"

That maddening shrug came again, but this time Dak recognized the pain behind the casual gesture. "He did what the rest of them do—got me drunk, paid the bar tab, and expected me to put out." Chase's fathomless brown eyes darkened to nearly black. "I might be known for cutting loose, but I don't fuck anyone I don't want to."

Rage surged through Dak. "He tried to rape you?"

"I didn't give him the chance. I'm not stupid."

That went a long way toward quelling the worst of Dak's violent urges. "The rest of them?"

38

Chase blinked. "Huh?"

"You said he did what the rest of them do. Who else has tried to rape you?"

The cub's mouth fell open. "It's not that they tried to rape me, just that they tried to get me drunk so I'd have sex with them."

"That's rape."

"Dak, it's okay. Some guys take being turned down better than others. Nobody got anything but a black eye or a broken nose, or one time, four scars from my claws. I know how to take care of myself." Chase stroked a caress down Dak's cheek.

Dak hadn't realized he'd released Chase's wrists. He closed his eyes and leaned into the caress. "I just don't like the idea of anyone hurting you."

"I know. You like to take care of people. It's why you became a cop."

Thinking back over his life, Dak realized Chase was right. There had always been someone who needed him to take care of them— brothers, friends, parents, and now, Chase.

Strong emotions obliterated Dak's ability to form words, so he kissed Chase. It was tender, an expression of thoughts that wouldn't form, and his cub's body relaxed, melding to his. What had begun as a caring gesture morphed as heat sparked between them.

Chase moaned, and his hands roamed Dak's body. Both cocks came to life. He reached between them to stroke his cub's cock, and Chase stroked Dak's.

The kiss went on and on, stealing his breath. Beneath him, Chase arched and writhed. Needing more control, Dak broke the kiss. He explored his way down Chase's body, kissing, licking, and nipping. Every touch seemed to drive Chase crazy, and Dak reveled in his cub's responsiveness.

Given what Chase had said, he knew he wasn't one more lover in a long line of men. Instinct told him Chase wasn't faking his innocence. Perhaps he wasn't a virgin, but he hadn't experienced all that much sexual activity. Chase might play around with flirting, but that's what cubs did—they played.

Dak spread Chase's legs wide and knelt between his legs. He licked the length of Chase's cock. Like him, it was long and lissome. Dak gripped the base and sucked the tip into his mouth.

Chase moaned and grabbed for Dak's head.

Dak lifted off. "Grip the spindles on the headboard. That's a good cub. Don't let go."

"I won't, Daddy." Chase's reply was half-whispered and half-mumbled, but Dak made it out just fine.

Power roared in his veins at Chase's use of that title. Dak had never considered using it before, but it fit, and he was pleased this sensitive little cub understood so much about him.

Dak resumed the blowjob. Keeping in mind how Chase had responded last time, he was careful with his cub's balls. Leaving off the blowjob, he tongued Chase's balls. The bear inside him needed more, so he licked the line of Chase's taint all the way back to his anus. He twirled his tongue around, memorizing the musky, salty flavor.

Chase's vocalizations became more and more ursine. Instead of words, he chuffed, moaned, grunted, and growled. Dak loved that he'd driven Chase to this primal place.

Kneeling up, he reached over to the nightstand for the lube.

Not letting go of the headboard, Chase watched Dak lube himself up. The cub's eyelids drooped with passion, and though his mouth was slack, his lips were still swollen from the blowjob he'd given earlier.

Dak rubbed the extra lubricant into Chase's sphincter. Inserting one finger, he massaged that tight muscle. Chase's breath caught and then exhaled in a low moan. Drizzling more lubricant in the area, Dak inserted a second finger to work and stretch the opening. Below him, Chase struggled to stay still. The purpled head of his cock throbbed against his abdomen. "Have you ever been taken from the front like this?"

Chase shook his head. His tongue darted out to lick his lower lip.

Dak couldn't imagine not seeing Chase's face the first time. He wanted Chase to understand this time—with Dak—was different from the quick, fervent hook-ups young cubs inevitably had as they navigated their early sexuality. "Keep your eyes open. I want to see you, and I want you to see me."

He positioned his cockhead at Chase's tight opening, and then he lifted his gaze. The feverish passion hadn't diminished, and the cub took shallow, anticipatory breaths. Dak cleaned his fingers with a wet wipe, and then he leaned over his cub.

He hiked Chase's bent legs up and out of the way. "This shouldn't hurt."

Chase grinned, a thoroughly cocky tilt to his lips. "It's okay if it does."

Gaze locked to his cub's, Dak pressed forward, and Chase exhaled. Stars exploded as Dak breached the outer ring and slid inside. A long, low moan sounded from deep inside Chase's throat, a guttural cry calling to Dak's primal nature. As Dak had commanded, Chase's gaze didn't waver.

Dak slid his cock all the way into his lover. "I'm in, sweetheart."

He dropped a kiss on Chase's lips, and then he went back for something slower and wetter. With his tongue wrapped up in Chase's mouth, he moved his hips.

Sensations overtook him, and he ripped his mouth from Chase's. "Cub, you feel so fucking good."

"Harder, Daddy, please." Chase arched, rubbing his turgid cock against Dak's stomach.

As he fucked his lover, Dak closed a hand around Chase's cock. He timed the movement of his hand with what his hips were doing. White-hot pleasure detonated in his core, and Dak came hard. He cried out, and Chase did as well. As he fell forward, he noted Chase's ejaculate coating his stomach. Ah, well. Now it coated his.

He rubbed their bodies together, spreading evidence of their passion between them.

Chase's arms came around Dak's shoulders. His cub held onto him, clinging as he shook. Low moans and whimpers still poured from him.

Dak lifted off his cub. "Are you too sore?"

Chase's hold tightened. "Stay how you are. Just for a minute, okay?"

Running his fingers through Chase's hair, Dak planted a string of kisses on his temple and forehead. "I'm here, my cub. I'm not going anywhere."

He must have slept. When he opened his eyes, he was half on top of Chase, and the lights blazed overhead. Yet he felt refreshed and disoriented.

Lifting up, he glanced at Chase to find the cub wide awake and regarding him with a sated smile. "How long was I out?"

"Few minutes. You're cute when you're asleep."

Dak peeled away, dragging Chase from the bed. "Only when I'm asleep?"

"Eh. I wouldn't exactly call you cute." Chase giggled. "Sexy, handsome, virile—those fit. Cute? Only when you're asleep."

Scooping Chase up in his arms, he carried him to the shower. "I'm going to wash you off, and then I'm going to fuck you again."

In the shower, Chase's playful nature came out full force. He soaped up his body and rubbed it against Dak's, getting in his way when he tried to clean himself and generally being bratty. When Dak tried to grab him, he slipped out of his grasp. Luckily it was a small shower and there was nowhere for Chase to go.

Dak pointed the shower spray at Chase to get rid of the soap, and then he snagged his prey. Under the warm flow of water, Dak trapped Chase's arms behind his back and kissed him senseless. Then he trailed kisses down Chase's neck. When he got to the base of Chase's neck, he partially shifted to bite his lover with bear teeth.

Chase went utterly limp and still, submitting to his alpha and the primal way he claimed him. Small whimpers escaped, the only evidence that Dak's bite hurt.

Between them, Chase's cock swelled.

Dak released the cub and bellowed in victory.

Chase was quiet while Dak toweled him dry and docile in his arms as he carried him back to bed. Dak held Chase as he claimed him once more. He fell asleep with Chase nestled in his embrace.

Chapter Seven

"Chase, did you finish the transmission on the Escape yet?" Arlen Fordline stood near the Honda SUV Chase was working on.

"Yep."

"I can't find the paperwork." An edge of irritation crept into Arlen's voice.

"I filed it." Chase hid the arrogant grin he couldn't squelch. He'd spent nearly every one of the past ten nights with Dak. Being with a Daddy bear had changed his outlook profoundly. For the first time in his life, he wanted to be responsible. No longer did he stubbornly insist he would only fix the cars; now he followed up with the billing and record entry.

Arlen shook his head. "Marlin said you've been doing your whole job since last week. Are you trying for a raise? Because we don't have any more money to pay you, kid. We'd have to raise our rates, and then customers would go elsewhere."

Chase looked up, surprised that Arlen thought he had an ulterior motive. But then he questioned Arlen's reasoning. Arlen and Marlin Fordline were Logan's fathers. They owned the garage where Chase worked. He was good enough to fix every car that came in, but he wasn't good enough to hang out with their son.

Rather than let ire and resentment color his response, he shrugged. "Do you not want me to do the paperwork? You're always yelling at me to do it. I thought I would do it. If that's not what you want, just let me know."

"No, I like it. Good job. Keep it up." Arlen patted him on the shoulder and returned to the front office.

Chase went back to the hoses he was reattaching, and he thought about what Arlen had said. There wasn't another garage in town, so there was nowhere else to take a vehicle to get it fixed. Then he thought about the future. Things between him and Dak had been pretty hot and heavy, and if they continued down this path, they'd want a future together. Eventually Chase would need to make more money in order to help support the kids he knew Dak would want to have.

"Are you thinking about that engine?" Logan's amused voice pulled Chase from his musings.

Chase threw a welcoming smile at his best friend. "What makes you think that?"

"It's the only time I've ever seen you take something seriously." Logan leaned against the front fender.

Frowning, Chase finished his task. "I'm serious about a lot of things. You tend to just be around when I'm blowing off steam."

"Fair enough." Logan shot a nervous glance toward the shop door. "Are you coming to The Bear's Den tonight? Albert Houser is back in town."

Two weeks ago, news like that would have made Chase swoon. Now Albert's name left a sour taste in his mouth. He wiped his hands on a towel, closed the hood, and then wiped away his greasy fingerprints. "I think I'm over The Bear's Den."

Logan lifted a brow. "There's nowhere else to go."

Rather than respond, Chase began the process of cleaning and stowing his tools. These didn't belong to the garage. They'd been a gift from his grandma when he'd earned his mechanic's certification. Nothing was more precious to him—except Grandma and Dak.

Logan watched for a few seconds. Then he snapped his fingers. "You're seeing someone. Who? Is it Albert? I saw you guys leave together a couple weeks ago, and you haven't been texting me much since then."

Not answering Logan was strangely satisfying to Chase. He threw a sly grin and continued with his task.

Logan rolled his eyes. "You've had a crush on Albert since high school."

As a rule, Chase didn't discuss his affairs with Logan. His best friend only wanted to hear about the surface details of his life, so he hadn't told Logan about how his association with Albert had soured. "I'm not dating Albert."

"Then who?" Logan smacked his arm. "I can't believe you're keeping this from me. I'm the one who told Albert you had a thing for him."

Outwardly, Chase gave no indication he'd heard anything. Inside, he seethed. Logan had dozens of friends, and he always seemed to make more everywhere he went. When people saw Chase coming, most of them adopted polite bearings that invited him to leave. "Yeah? When was this?"

Logan shrugged. "My dads had people over a few weeks ago. Albert came. We got to talking, and I remembered how you had a crush on him in high school. So I told him he had a chance with you."

The Fordlines held frequent gatherings. Arlen and Marlin liked to entertain. Chase had never once been invited. Only a week ago, Chase hadn't questioned why Logan wouldn't stand up to his fathers and defend their friendship. He hadn't questioned why Logan kept the truth of their association secret. He'd merely accepted his place on the periphery of Logan's world.

Today that bothered him. For the first time, he wasn't satisfied with the crumbs of Logan's friendship.

Shoring up his courage, Chase flashed a maddening grin. "I'm not seeing Albert." He picked up his toolbox and set it in the trunk of his car.

Logan headed him off. "Is he married?"

"What? No." Shock made him answer. The first man who'd broken his heart had been married. Chase had kept quiet about their affair. His lover had promised to get a divorce, but it never happened. Chase had learned his lesson the way hard way, and he'd sworn off married men, which Logan knew, so he didn't understand why Logan asked that question. "I never said I was seeing anyone, just that I didn't want to go to The Bear's Den. If you want to hang out, then invite me over for pizza and a movie."

Logan's eyes widened. "Chase, I can't. You know I can't."

He'd known what Logan's answer would be, but he needed to give his so-called best friend one more chance. "Look, we're twenty-three. If you don't have the balls to be friends with me in public, then there's no reason for us to be friends in private."

The color drained from Logan's face. "You don't mean that."

In all the years they'd been friends, Chase had accepted Logan's conditions without questioning them. Now he understood how much he'd sold himself short. He scooted Logan away from his trunk and closed the lid. "I mean it. Now, if you'll excuse me, I have to write up the report for the Honda so I can be finished for the day."

He left Logan with a pensive pout on his face.

At home, he fried chicken and made cornbread with Simone.

"You're happy," she observed as they sat down for their meal.

"I am." He grinned, and this time he didn't need to be cocky or arrogant. It was simply joyous. "I'm in love."

Simone matched his smile. "With Deputy Dak Freeman. He's a nice man."

Chase had talked about Dak to Simone, but he hadn't introduced them. "He's off tomorrow. Maybe I'll invite him over to meet you."

She waved a hand. "We met today. Since you've been spending so much time with your young man, I made it my business to see for myself if he was good enough for you."

Chase reached across the table and took her hand. "Grandma, you are an amazing woman, and I love you dearly. What did you think?" He wasn't afraid she wouldn't like Dak. There wasn't anything about him that wasn't lovable.

"I thought he was very much in love with you. He has a good head on his shoulders. He's solid. Strong. Like your father." She squeezed his hand and went back to shredding her chicken.

The comparison brought tears to his eyes, mostly because Simone always spoke of his father in glowing terms. "I'm glad you like him."

"Male brown bears have cubs in four-to-five months."

Chase blinked at Simone. "Okay."

"Have you and Dak been using protection?"

This was not a conversation he wanted to have with his grandmother. "Grandma!"

"You're of breeding age, sweetheart, as is Dak, and he's one incredibly virile male. Did you not pay attention to sexual education in school?"

Chase hadn't cared about any class except auto shop, but that didn't mean he'd blown off everything. Simone would have killed him for anything under a C. "I paid attention." All the sex he had prior to Dak had been safe.

"Then you're using condoms?"

"I'm not talking about this with you."

At his continued obfuscation, she rolled her eyes and snorted. "I'll take that as a no. Well, then, watch for the signs."

"Signs?" In the heat of the moment, he hadn't thought about any of that, and in the other moments, he'd been too busy basking in the afterglow.

"Mood swings, increased sensitivity, increased appetite, increased sexual urges—the signs." Simone's grin showed Chase where he'd learned such flippant behavior. "You're an omega. That means you're the one who'll carry the cubs. I'm glad you're not going out drinking tonight."

She'd given him plenty to think about, and in an hour, she was asleep on her favorite chair while the theme song to her game show played on the TV.

Chase packed up the leftovers and took dinner to Dak at the station. He sailed into the familiar place to find Evan Chillwell manning the counter. "Hi, Deputy Chillwell. How are you?"

Chillwell smiled, a look that warmed up his whole face. "Are you turning yourself in before you do anything ill-advised?"

Heat crept up Chase's cheeks. "I brought dinner for Dak."

"Aww, that's sweet. Dak's on a call. Don't know when he'll be back."

Chase wasn't sure if he should wait around.

Evan pulled out a chair. "You play gin? I need to practice. My sister kicks my ass on a weekly basis."

"I've never played."

"Fantastic. That means I get to win."

Gin, it turned out, had a lot in common with poker. Chase had grown up playing with Simone, the two of them betting toothpicks or chores. Chillwell didn't want to wager with a beginner. He was a quiet player who narrowed his eyes and chuffed when he didn't like his cards. It didn't take long for Chase to win more hands than he lost.

An hour later, the deputy threw his cards on the counter between them. "It's official—I suck at this."

Chase shuffled the deck. "You have tells."

Chillwell opened and closed his mouth. "What are they?"

Laughing, Chase shook his head. "Rule number one in poker— never enlighten an opponent."

The corners of Chillwell's mouth turned down. Before he could reply, the chimes on the door sounded.

Both men looked to see who had arrived. Upon recognizing Dak, Chase squealed. He leaped across the station and threw himself in Dak's arms.

Dak caught him. "This is a pleasant surprise." He pressed his lips against Chase's.

The cub melted against his Daddy.

Chillwell shrugged into his jacket and reached for his hat. "If you don't need me, I'll do some patrol on my way home."

Dak released Chase. "It's a quiet night."

"It usually is." Chillwell lifted his chin in Chase's direction. "Thanks for tonight. See you."

As the door closed behind the deputy, Dak perched his hands on his hips and faced Chase. "What's he thanking you for?"

"I don't know. I brought you dinner, but you weren't here, so I played cards with Deputy Chillwell." Chase leaned his chest against Dak's larger one and walked his fingers along Dak's shoulder. "After you eat, I thought maybe I could hang around until you get off work?"

Dak slid his arms around Chase and captured his mouth for a searing kiss.

Sighing in the embrace, he gave himself over to his alpha.

After far too short of a time, Dak broke away. "I smell fried chicken."

Chase bounced to where he'd stowed the bag full of food. "Cornbread and potatoes too."

Shifting burned a lot of calories, and so food was important to a bear. They ate anything and everything, and Chase had found that Dak especially loved starches and sweets.

Dak locked the front door and put out the sign for people to ring the doorbell or call an emergency number. "Let's take this into the break room." With his hand on Chase's lower back, Dak guided his omega to a small room behind the reception area.

While Dak ate, Chase chattered about the cars he'd fixed that day. Dak tucked into the food with both hands, not seeming to hear a word Chase was saying.

Chase wondered if they'd come to the point in their relationship where they ignored each other. He'd heard it was a thing that happened to some couples, but he didn't think it would happen to him—especially not this soon.

"Dak? Am I boring you?"

Dak finished chewing and washed it down with a swig of water. "Not at all. You're an excellent cook. I can't remember the last time I had anything this good in my mouth."

Chase's cock jumped at the opportunity, but he ignored it. Heat crept into his cheeks, and he smiled. "I love to cook. I've never cooked for anyone except my grandma before."

The smile curving Dak's full lips was reward enough for the small but significant confession. "Did you get the belts changed on that Honda?"

"Yeah. I did the paperwork as well. Arlen stuck around. I think he was shocked I was actually doing the paperwork." Chase broke off, thinking about Arlen's comment about not getting a raise. "He said something that bothered me, though. He said they didn't make enough at the garage to give me a raise. But now that I'm doing the billing for my jobs, I'm wondering if that's true. They upcharge the parts, and then they bill for my time. What they bill and what I get paid aren't the same thing."

"That's common," Dak said. "There's overhead, like rent or taxes, and maintenance costs to keep a place running."

"But shouldn't that come out of the upcharge on the parts or be a separate fee? They charge other fees."

"I don't know, Chase. Are you thinking of opening up your own place?"

Though he'd rejected the idea before, this was the first time he'd seriously thought about it. "Maybe. I can fix anything, so I wouldn't just do cars. I can have a general repair shop—lawnmowers, vacuum cleaners, household appliances, and cars."

A fierce pride gleamed in Dak's eyes. "Your motto can be that you fix everything."

Chase lost himself for several long moments, dreaming about what his life could be like. He could close down for two weeks every summer and go on vacation. He'd love to shift for a couple of weeks and roam the woods in bear form. It had been too long since he'd cut loose like that. Drinking to oblivion was a poor substitute for spending time in his bear form.

When his mind returned from the short trip, he found Dak watching him. He'd finished the food, and now he sat back in his chair and studied Chase.

As was his habit, he covered up his self-consciousness with a brazen grin. "See something you like?"

Dak patted his lap. "Come here, my cub."

The break room was equipped with a kitchenette, a round table, and four chairs. Chase rounded the table and perched on Dak's powerful thighs. "Yes, Daddy?"

The kiss was expected, as was the hand running up his thigh and the fingers digging into his hip. With a contented gasp, Chase submitted to the man for whom he'd fallen. Dak deepened the kiss, robbing Chase of breath and reason. When he felt Dak's hand stroke his growing erection through his pants, Chase gasped.

Dak caught the noise in his mouth, and with a possessive growl, he broke the kiss. "Let's play a game."

"What kind of game?" Thinking back to the card game he'd played with Deputy Chillwell, he envisioned strip poker. That would be fun to lose.

"I'm going to arrest you."

A sentimental thrill ran through Chase, and his erection came fully alive. "That's how we met." With a grin, he leapt to his feet. "Do you want me to resist arrest?"

Dak rose. His blue eyes brightened with anticipation. "No. You were cooperative both times. I want you to do what comes naturally."

"Yes, Daddy. What am I being arrested for?"

"Indecent exposure. Drop your pants."

Chase unbuckled his belt before tackling his fly. With a push, the pants slid down his thighs, and the underwear followed. "Deputy Sex God, if you're going to arrest me, I may never pull them back up." To emphasize his point, he stroked his cock.

Dak's gaze heated him, sending a thrill through Chase's entire body. He had no intention of stopping. He knew the moment Dak pinpointed his intention. "Oh, no, you don't."

The room whirled, and Chase found himself bent over the table. "Oh, yes, Deputy Sex God. Do me like this."

Cold metal encircled his wrists, and the familiar clicks of the handcuffs locking filled the room. "Spread your legs."

With the pants binding his knees, he could only go so far. Dak's hands patted him down, but this was wholly different from what he'd done before. Instead of quick, businesslike touches, he moved slowly, somehow claiming every inch of Chase's body. Dak's fingers pressed while his palms caressed, and by the time he slid a hand between Chase's legs and cupped his balls, Chase was ready to explode.

"Oh, Deputy, that feels so good. If this is what prison is like, lock me up now."

Behind him, Dak chuckled. "Lock you up? That's definitely part of the plan."

Dak's touch fell away much too soon, and a whine rumbled in Chase's throat. He wanted to beg to have it back, but he knew Dak had a plan, so he forced himself to swallow the plea.

Dak gripped the back of Chase's neck, hauling him upright. Then he pushed him forward, out of the break room, through the station, and into the lockup where two cells waited. Chase had occupied each of them at one point in his life.

Outside of the closed cell, Dak released one of the cuffs. Before Chase could question that move, he found himself handcuffed to a horizontal bar that ran above his head. In short order, his free arm was secured the same way. Now he was bound with his arms above him and his pants around his ankles where they had fallen during the walk through the station. In front of him, he could see the bars of the cell and the off-white cinderblock in the back of the small cell.

His cock had never been so hard before.

"This place is soundproof." Dak's breath tickled on Chase's neck. "No one will hear you scream."

"I'm going to scream?" For the first time, Chase worried about what was going to happen.

"Beg, scream, moan—you're going to be loud." With his fingertips, Dak traced a light caress down Chase's back. "I'm going to do things to you, Chase. The next time you think to expose yourself in public, you're going to remember this consequence."

Chase's mind spun, searching for ideas as to what Dak could possibly do. Spanking and fucking came to mind, both of which Chase liked. However he didn't think Dak would limit himself to just those two things. Though he'd promised to tie Chase up a few times, he hadn't done it. Their time together had been marked by intense bouts of passion neither one of them sought to control.

Something cold pressed to his scrotum. With a bellow, Chase tried to wiggle away, but there was nowhere to go. "What the fuck is that? Ice? You're going to make my cock go soft."

The hard piece of cold hell moved around his balls and down the length of his softening cock. This move seemed counter to the point of the whole exercise.

Chase looked down and sighed. A perfectly good erection had been wasted.

Dak pulled his hips. "Take a step back."

Chase complied, which meant now his arms were stretched as far as they'd go, and he was bent over a little. He gripped the metal bars for support.

Dak filled the space, kneeling in front of Chase. Before his cock could rejoice, Dak wrapped a piece of small-gauged rope around his penis and scrotum. He did this several times, binding his man parts in a bundle.

Having Dak on his knees with that expression—the one promising pleasure and demanding submission—did things for Chase. He found it hot no matter what else was going on.

"Deputy? Why are you handcuffing my junk?"

Dak gripped Chase's cock in his strong, hot hand. Stirrings flared brighter, and his cock once again lengthened. Dak opened his mouth and sucked Chase's manhood inside.

Blood rushed to the area, and Chase hissed. It felt great, but it also stung a little. He cried out at the unexpected sensation. "Fuck, that's weird."

In response, Dak increased his pace.

Chase wanted to thrust his hips, but he was too overwhelmed to move. Dak's hot mouth felt so fucking good, and the sight of his head bobbing on Chase's cock further fueled passion's fire. Flames licked his insides, and his core tightened. His balls were already drawn up—and tied at the base. Normally Chase would have come by now, but his balls were having a hard time cresting that mountaintop.

The loud sounds pouring from him took on a desperate edge, and that's when Dak stopped.

He stood, petting the short hairs at the base of Chase's neck. "It's going to be a while before you come, prisoner of mine. That rope will make sure your erection doesn't wane. It's going to be difficult to climax, and when you come, it's going to both hurt and feel incredible." He drew a fingertip down Chase's temple. "I'm not going to release the cuffs until you come."

Chase's mind reeled. "Dak," he whined. "Don't be cruel. It was just a little public indecency—nothing too bad."

Dak smacked a kiss on Chase's cheek. "Begging already. I like it."

While Chase didn't mind begging, Dak's description of what would happen didn't put him at ease. If anything, it sharpened the tumult of feelings freewheeling through his body.

Dak disappeared behind him again, and coldness pressed to Chase's anus. Before he could consider whether he wanted it to happen, Dak inserted a small, round cube of ice into his ass. More followed.

Chase's insides cooled, the freezing water fighting with his body heat in a test of wills. He shivered and moaned. His erection did not wane.

"Hold those inside while I punish you." Dak's hand connected with the cheek of Chase's ass. The blows alternated. They weren't hard, but they got the job done.

Chase clenched to keep the ice from slipping out, which made the spanking sting more. He recalled the last time Dak had done this, how the pain had morphed into pleasure and how the entire process had nourished a kernel of peace in his core.

The spanking went on and on, generating heat on his skin in direct contrast to the chill in his rectum. Loud sounds of skin-on-skin filled the air. Soon the sting morphed to pleasure as endorphins flooded his system.

Dak stopped. He fisted a handful of Chase's hair. "How are you doing, prisoner? Are you still with me?"

"Yes, Deputy." Chase was aware enough to remember the scene they were playing. He channeled a bit of the sexual frustration and directed it at Dak. "Are you going to just play around? What's wrong—can't get it up? Awww—poor impotent deputy."

Dak's brows shot skyward. "Impotent? Oh, my prisoner cub, you've just earned a harsher punishment."

With that, Dak slid the belt from the loops in Chase's pants. He folded it in half. Chase heard the leather whistle through the air, and it landed across his buttocks with a loud snap. It took a moment for the sting to register.

Tears pricked Chase's eyes, not from grief or upset, but from the potency of the sting. Before he could cry out, another blow landed. On the third one, a guttural bellow issued from Chase's depths.

Dak showed no mercy. He went after Chase's ass, thighs, and calves. Chase's brain ceased keeping track. It stalled, and Chase was left with only the sting, the heat, and the way his entire body came alive.

Barely aware when it stopped, he noted the way his skin buzzed. Dak drew a finger up his leg, the sensation multiplied due to the sensitivity in his skin. It took him a few passes to realize Dak was using ice. It created a curious juxtaposition, and Chase's confused nerve endings short-circuited in a riot of pleasure.

Vaguely Chase wondered if the ice in his ass had melted, but he didn't much care. The things Dak did took away his ability to think and reason.

The tip of Dak's cock nudged his sphincter, and a shock of anticipation ran through Chase, surprising him with violent intensity. A gasp escaped his lips.

Already lubed up, the alpha's cock breached the opening easily. In keeping with his rough treatment, Dak reamed Chase, slamming all the way inside.

Chase cried out at the pleasure-pain, and he gripped the bars harder. His cock throbbed and the skin on his backside tingled from hip to ankle. Sweat trickled down his back, and Dak pounded into his ass, rubbing over his prostate and sending shards of pleasure through his dick.

"Daddy, oh, Daddy, please. Yes, harder." Words, pleas and nonsense syllables, whispered from Chase. Having given himself over to Dak, he didn't bother to control anything.

Then Dak's hand encircled Chase's cock. "You're going to come, my prisoner cub. I want to hear you."

Pain pricked at the base of his cock, but it felt so fucking wonderful that Chase changed his opinion of the sensation. "Yes, Daddy."

Desperate noises and moans growled from deep in his chest as Dak awakened Chase's inner bear. Dak's pace increased as he fucked his cock into Chase and milked the omega's cock. His teeth sank into Chase's shoulder, sharp pinpricks that didn't quite break the skin.

Lost in a sea of strange, sensual pleasures, Chase's orgasm was a tidal wave claiming him and making him part of the sea. He screamed and bucked, fighting the hot depth even as it forced him deeper.

Left with no choice, he surrendered to the vast ocean of bliss.

When he became aware of his surroundings, he found himself in Dak's arms. His alpha sat on the floor of the jail with Chase on his lap.

"Shhh." Dak brushed his fingers through Chase's hair as he clucked soothing sounds punctuated by kisses pressed to Chase's forehead. "I'm here, cub. Daddy's got you."

Chapter Eight

"Grandma, did you get paper napkins?"

Dak paused on the porch, listening to Chase's voice drift through the screen door. His cub was nervous even though he knew Dak and Simone had already met, and they two were determined to love each other because they both loved Chase.

"Chase, get away from the table. It's perfect, not that your deputy will notice. He only has eyes for you."

Imagining Simone's gnarled finger wagging at Chase, Dak swallowed back a laugh. He knocked on the aluminum door frame, and the conversation inside hushed.

Chase appeared at the door, a flirty smile tugging at his lips, and he pushed the door open. "Glad you could come over."

Dak noted the care Chase had taken with his appearance. The omega wore linen pants and a light peach shirt that made him look like he'd come from a walk on the beach. His hair, carefully coiffed so his bangs lifted straight up and pitched back in gentle waves, was strategically messy to give it a windblown look.

Slipping past his omega into the house, Dak slid an arm around Chase's waist and pulled him closer for a kiss. "Thanks for inviting me."

Dak had also dressed to impress. He wore the dressiest jeans he owned, which he paired with a blue plaid, button-down shirt that brought out the pale blue of his irises.

Across the living room, Simone waited. Dak had no idea how old the woman was, but he estimated her to be at least ninety. Nothing in any files or records he'd traced had identified Simone Longfellow as anything but a relative who had appeared after Chase's parents had vanished.

He crossed to her and held out a hand. She put hers in it, her soft skin almost translucent. Yet she exuded strength, and he knew it came from her spirit because her flesh was definitely on the weak side.

"Simone, it's good to see you again. Thanks for allowing me into your home."

Her eyes narrowed, and Dak waited patiently while the elderly woman studied him. He had no idea what she saw or what she was thinking, but he knew that her opinion mattered to Chase—and so it mattered to him.

At long last, she nodded. "You'll do."

Not knowing how to take that, he smiled at her approval. Then he fished a tin of sardines from his pocket. "These are for you."

Gifting sardines was serious business among bears. It signified respect of the highest order and a desire for lifelong friendship.

Unsurprised, Simone smiled as she accepted it. "Thank you."

Dak glanced over to find Chase watching him with misty eyes. The show of vulnerability set off his alpha side, and Dak put his arm around Chase. He leaned close. "Are you okay?"

Chase nodded and wiped away a stray tear. "That was sweet of you."

Simone rolled her eyes. "I'm starving. Let's eat."

They followed Simone, walking slowly as Simone shuffled along.

"Did you cook?" Dak asked Simone. "It smells divine."

Scents of garlic and marinara sauce permeated the air. Chase flashed a grin. "I cooked."

Simone paused in the kitchen and turned to face the pair. "I'm not much of a cook. Chase started when he was about eight. He'd watch cooking shows, and then he'd want to make the dish. I helped him at first, but I couldn't keep up. It turned out I was more of a hindrance. I can make the basics, and I'm an okay assistant."

Chase released Dak to kiss Simone's cheek. "You're my inspiration, which is enough." Then he pulled out her chair.

Dak watched as Chase helped his grandmother sit down, and Dak realized the old woman's health was quite frail. In his head, he revised his plans to ask Chase to move in with him. He'd need to get a place large enough to accommodate Simone as well. The both of them could take care of Simone.

A knock on the door sounded as Chase brought food to the table. Chase paused in the midst of setting down a pan of lasagna. He frowned at Simone. "Did you invite a date?"

Her laugh tinkled across the room, filling the space with a delightful sound. "Oh, you. No, I'm not expecting anyone."

Chase sniffed the air. Dak was closer to the door, and he couldn't catch the scent of whomever was there, so he figured Chase couldn't either. Chase finished setting down the pan. "Dak, can you get the bread out of the broiler while I see who's at the door?"

"Sure."

Dak was bent over, retrieving the cookie sheet of garlic bread, when raised voices came through from the living room.

"Oh, dear," Simone said. "Logan's here."

Chase had told Dak about Logan, his best friend, and Dak didn't have a positive view of the man who professed friendship only when it was convenient. Dak set the hot sheet on the stove and headed for the living room.

Logan Fordline was a handsome man. Like Chase, he had a tall, lithe build, brown eyes, and blond hair. Unlike Chase, Logan's body wasn't honed from days of physical labor. Logan was fit, but softer.

When Dak entered the room, Logan's hard glare landed on him, but his words were directed at Chase. "This is why you can't be friends with me anymore?" Logan lifted his chin, and threw the next question at Dak. "Did you order him not to hang out with me?"

Dak was well aware some alphas set rules like that for their omegas, but he wasn't the sort. The only rule he'd insisted upon was Chase not drink to excess so he didn't do stupid things and get in trouble with the law. To his way of thinking, it was a reasonable restriction.

He went closer, lending strength to his cub with his proximity. "Chase is free to have all the friends he wants."

Logan's heated gaze shot back to Chase. "I'm here, and I'm not leaving."

Chase squared his shoulders, stepping up to his sometimes-friend. "I didn't invite you over, and I'm not inviting you in."

"You said I was always welcome here." Logan's lips pressed together, an attempt at bravado.

"Yeah, like ten years ago. Yet this is the first time you've come here. I didn't know you knew where I lived." Chase inhaled sharply, widening his eyes dramatically. "Did you know you were on the wrong side of town? Poor people live here, Logan. Quick—get out before you're recognized."

Red flamed Logan's cheeks, but determination flashed in his eyes. "I'm not leaving until you talk to me."

Dak set a hand on Chase's shoulder. "There's plenty of food. Logan, why don't you join us for lunch? Chase made lasagna, and I'd rather eat it before it gets cold than listen to you two argue at the door."

Logan slid past Chase, shooting him a triumphant look.

Chase glared at Dak. Before he could say anything, Dak said, "I'd like to spend some time getting to know Logan for myself." He fanned a caress down Chase's cheek. "I'm on your side, cub. Always."

The fight went out of Chase. The omega's reaction compounded the intense love Dak felt for Chase. He pulled him close for a firm kiss, and then they joined Logan and Simone in the kitchen.

Simone pushed on the table to rise, and Chase flew into action as soon as he saw her. "Grandma, I'll get it. You stay where you are. Dak, can you serve the lasagna?"

They'd seated him at the head of the table, and Dak understood the symbolism of the placement. He set to work carving the lasagna while Chase plated the bread and brought over a place setting for their unexpected guest.

Simone's eyes sidled to Logan every now and again, but she mostly ignored him. That act spoke volumes.

"Dak, Chase tells me you're from Forrest Hills originally."

"Yes. My fathers still live there, but my brothers have scattered." He served everyone, and Chase passed around the plate of garlic bread.

Across the short rectangle of the table, Logan glared as he cut a bite of food. "If your family is there, why did you leave?"

Chase frowned. "Logan, don't be rude. It's none of your business."

It was a question Chase had never asked, and Dak felt his omega deserved an answer. However he didn't want to go into the gory details in front of Logan, so he settled on a half-truth. "There were no openings in law enforcement. I knew when I chose this field I'd have to relocate. When the job opened up in Bear's Cove, I jumped at the chance."

Logan shot a look at Chase. "I'll bet you did."

This wasn't going the way Dak expected. Chase didn't want Logan there, and Logan's jealousy over Chase's happiness made no sense. Simone and Chase didn't need to be subjected to this kind of hostility in their own home. Dak rose and squared his shoulders. Then he rounded the table and closed a hand around Logan's arm. "You need to learn some manners. Come with me."

Logan didn't come willingly, so Dak dragged him from the room. He dragged him through the living room and out to the front lawn. Once he had Logan away from the Longfellows, he released his hold.

Logan jerked away and regarded him with a ferocious light in his eyes. "What the fuck is your problem? Just because you're a deputy doesn't mean you get to treat me like this."

Dak stood his ground. He wasn't there as the law; he was Chase's alpha. "My problem, Logan, is that you want nothing to do with Chase until it's convenient. I'm not sure what you think you're going to accomplish with this stunt, but it's not going to repair your friendship with Chase. He's a wonderful person. Anyone would be happy to count him as a friend. He can and will do better than you."

Malice glinted in Logan's eyes. "No, he can't. Nobody in this town wants anything to do with Chase Longfellow. He's tainted, and every person in this town steers clear of him. They might be nice to his face, but nobody wants him around. Just like everyone else I know, I'm not allowed to be friends with him because my fathers are afraid he'll get me killed. We all know what happened to his parents. Bad luck follows him around, and that shit is contagious."

He lifted his gaze to peer over Dak's shoulder, and Dak suddenly became aware of Chase standing at the front door. "I'm all you got, Chase. You ever wonder why nobody else wanted to hang out with you? It's because they're scared. Even me. Maybe I was a shitty friend, but I tried. Even though everyone told me to stay the fuck away from you, I did the best I could."

Next his glare returned to Dak. Unshed tears glistened in Logan's eyes. He poked a finger in Dak's chest. "You're going to lose everything if you stay with him. People are already talking about how they don't want you to respond to calls, how you're tainted too. Maybe you love him, but he'll destroy you, just like he did to me."

Dak had no idea how Logan had been destroyed, but he responded to the cruelty of Logan's assertions. He wished Chase hadn't followed them out front. He wished he'd done a better job of protecting his omega from hearing what Logan said.

He closed the distance, his low growl not needing much to carry to the person who'd been Chase's only friend for so long. "You're a fucking coward. If you cared about Chase at all, it wouldn't matter what everyone else thought. If you loved him as a friend should, you would know all that talk about bad luck is bullshit. He lived through a terrible tragedy, and with the love of his grandmother, he held onto his optimism, compassion, and vibrancy. You came here today to chase me away so you could continue treating him like shit, you sniveling bastard, and you're pissed off because it's not going to happen."

Though Logan's mouth tightened and the sheen of tears in his eyes burned with rage, his glare didn't waver. When Dak finished, Logan stalked back to his car.

Dak returned to the house. Chase held the door open, but his gaze pointed to the floor.

He couldn't have his cub thinking Logan had made an impact. With a finger under Chase's chin, he urged the omega's face upward. The anguish in Chase's face echoed as pain in Dak's heart. This was his fault. "I'm sorry about that. I thought maybe the fact he showed up here meant he was ready to be a real friend. I was wrong."

Chase's gaze flittered away, and he shrugged. "You don't owe me an apology."

"Look at me." Dak waited until Chase complied. "I do. You're mine, Chase, mine to love and protect, and I failed you today. I don't take that lightly."

"It's my fault." Simone's thin voice interrupted anything further Dak might have said. She hobbled into the room and fell into a well-worn recliner. "I should have taken him away from here years ago."

"Grandma, it's not your fault either." Chase tucked a blanket around Simone's legs. "It's nobody's fault. I've lied to you for years about having friends. I hated anything that might disappoint you, so I lied about going to the park to hang out with friends. I went to the park, but I played alone. Logan was all I had, and he forced me to keep our friendship a secret."

Dak guided Chase to the sofa. He sat next to his lover and pulled him into his arms. "You told me how Logan treated you. I invited him to lunch even though you were trying to make him leave."

Chase patted Dak's cheek. "You meant well."

"So did you." Simone sighed. "Chase, I never told you who I am. I never told you how I came to be here."

In Dak's arms, Chase stiffened. "You're my grandma, and you took me in when my parents died."

Chase was trying to be strong, but he couldn't quite hide the tremor in his voice. Dak wanted like hell to salve the wound, but he didn't know how to right past wrongs—things that had happened decades before he'd come to Bear's Cove. And so he held his cub, lending strength any way he could.

Simone shook her head. "Chase, I love you with everything I am. I meant to die years ago, but I kept going because you needed me."

Tears pooled in the old woman's rheumy eyes and dripped down her cheeks. She waved away Chase when he tried to go to her, and she grabbed a handful of tissue from the side table next to her recliner.

"I'm not quite your grandmother. I'm your mother's grandmother. She was human, as am I, and when she fell in love with your father, her parents didn't approve. They had a falling out, and I opened my home to her. I covered for her, you see. She never actually came to live with me. She ran away with your father, and I held her parents at bay. It was easy at first because they were angry and were punishing her with silence."

Simone paused, her breaths coming quickly. Dak wondered if that was due to her emotions or to her physical frailty. Chase waited patiently for his grandmother to continue, and Dak did the same.

After a moment, she sighed again. "Lea was a gentle girl, the kind of person who had a kind word for everyone. Everyone she met couldn't help but love her. When she brought William around, I knew she'd met someone who completed her. He understood her. He nurtured her. He cared for her. He loved her with his entire heart and soul. But he was a bear shifter, and where we were raised, bear shifters were hunted. They're circus attractions, or they're kept in cages for scientists to experiment upon. It's horrible."

Dak knew these things about the human world. That's why bear settlements were enshrouded in magical mists and protected with wards that deterred humans from noticing they existed. Judging from the way Chase stiffened in his arms, the cub hadn't known. Dak soothed Chase with a caress down his arm and a rumbling vocalization his father had used whenever Dak had been upset as a child.

"Lea and William had you, and years passed. I hated the silence between Lea and her parents, so one day I went to my daughter's house, and I told them Lea was married. Before I could tell them about the beautiful life they'd built and about you, my son-in-law stormed out of the room. My daughter told me that she never wanted to see me again. They threw me out."

Palpable anger ran through Chase's body, and his paws shifted. Surprised at the cub's lack of control, he gripped Chase by the back of the neck and forced him to meet Dak's gaze. "Cub, breathe. You control the shift. It doesn't control you." He set Chase's paws on his chest. "Match my breathing. Concentrate on remaining in human form."

Seconds passed, and Chase's paws morphed back into hands.

Simone nodded. "I didn't know what to teach him. He's so mild-mannered, so much like Lea, that it has never really been a problem."

Dak nodded. "I'm here. I'll fill in the gaps."

"Good." Her fond smile faded. "Lea's parents found her. They came here—because I told them where they'd gone—and they murdered Lea and William."

Having seen the files, Dak protested. "You don't know that. Bodies were never found. Evidence of humans having been on the scene wasn't found."

Simone set a fist over her heart. "I know it here." Her eyes flashed with a million kinds of regret and anger. "That's why I came here in the first place—I suspected the worst. The police said the same thing you did, and then they gave Chase to me. I stayed here because Lea wanted Chase raised here. She loved Bear's Cove. And Chase would have been in danger in the human world."

Silence rang in Dak's ears, and he didn't seek to break it. Chase needed time to let Simone's confession sink in. He'd officially lost his best—and only—friend today, and now he'd learned why the entire town shunned him. Humans and shifters didn't get along because humans considered shifters to be animals. Conversely, shifters viewed humans as freaks of nature. Though it was acceptable to marry one as long as they were omegas, their offspring were often regarded as half-breeds.

It was difficult enough to fit in without heaping all kinds of prejudice on top of the matter.

Dak rubbed circles on Chase's back. He thought about the lack of evidence proving humans had been on the scene. Even the file claimed they'd found nothing, which was strange if Lea had been human.

It was a fresh line of thought to pursue in the cold case.

After a long time, a pathetic version of a laugh coughed from Chase. "Dak, I'll understand if you want to cut and run."

Caught off-guard because that hadn't been the drift of his thoughts, Dak started. "I love you. I'm not going anywhere." Then he sighed. It seemed to be going around lately. "You know, not everyone avoids you. After I arrested you the second time, Evan sat me down to tell me to cut you some slack. He said you were a good person who caught some tough breaks. He showed me your file."

The ghost of a smile appeared on Chase's face. "He sent you to the garage that day."

"Cord did. He wanted me to get to know the real you."

"He probably didn't expect you to ask me out."

Dak shrugged. "He didn't seem surprised when I did."

"I didn't find out until later, but a lot of William's friends abandoned him when he married a human." Simone's rasp reminded them they weren't alone. "Bears are just as prejudiced as humans, but at least I knew they wouldn't harm Chase. So I bought this little house. It seemed the perfect size for an old lady to raise her great-grandson." She blinked, and more tears fell down her cheeks. "Until a couple years ago, I didn't even know there were other bear settlements we could have gone to. I'm so sorry, Chase."

Her apology did something to Chase. He sat up straight and huffed out a breath. "Grandma, you did the best you could. I don't remember my parents, but you managed to keep them alive in my memory. You didn't know my father very well, but you loved him, and you nurtured my love for my parents. And I adore you. Maybe you lied to me, but you did it out of love. You were there for me when I needed you most, and you've been here for me every day since. I love you so much."

Simone seemed almost to float out of her chair, so great was the burden she'd set free.

Dak gave Chase a push toward Simone, and his cub bolted across the room. He knelt on the floor and threw his arms around his grandmother's waist, burying his face in her lap. Dak sat back and gave them space.

Moments passed, and then Simone tapped Chase's shoulder. "Chase, we didn't eat yet, and I'm famished."

Chase lumbered to his feet. "I'll heat up the food." He turned to Dak. "Can you help Grandma into the kitchen?"

"Sure." Dak didn't hurry Simone as she took her time getting up. He offered an arm and a hand, which she accepted.

Once she was on her feet, she reached up to set a hand on Dak's cheek. "I know he's in good hands now."

An understanding passed between them. Responsibility for Chase now belonged to Dak. He gladly accepted it.

Chapter Nine

Chase

Chase woke up entangled in a sheet and Dak's warm embrace. Yesterday had been intense. After lunch, Dak had spent the day at his house, chatting with him and Simone through dinner. Once the dinner dishes had been washed, she'd shooed them both out the door.

"You need time together," she'd said. "And this old lady wants to watch her shows in peace."

And so Chase had spent the night at Dak's house. He slipped out of bed.

"Where are you going, little cub?"

"I was going to make breakfast."

Dak rolled to his back and stretched. Chase's gaze was drawn to the growing tent in the sheet, and his stomach growled for a different kind of protein.

Crawling back into bed, he drew the sheet down Dak's massive chest, revealing that vast expanse of chiseled muscle. Dak's hips came next, and Chase had to lift the sheet to expose that thick cock.

He checked to see if Dak's eyes were opened or closed, and he found his alpha watching him through heavy-lidded eyes. Saliva pooled in Chase's mouth, and when he slid Dak's erection into his mouth, he had enough to take it all the way in.

Dak let him set the pace. Chase knew what Dak liked first thing in the morning, so he bobbed his head quickly. Normally Dak let him work in peace, but this morning, his alpha lifted Chase to kneel over Dak's mouth. Warm wetness closed around Chase's cock as Dak sucked him deep.

With a moan, Chase got serious. In no time at all, warm semen bathed the back of Chase's throat. He swallowed it down as he climaxed in Dak's mouth.

Then he sat back and smacked his lips. "Thank you, Daddy. Now I'll make breakfast."

He threw on his pants from the day before and headed into the kitchen. As he tossed together fixings for an omelet, he listened to the beautiful music of Dak moving through the small condo. Water ran, and he heard Dak's phone ring. He listened to the bass murmur of Dak's voice even though he couldn't make out any of the words. It didn't matter.

For the first time in his life, Chase was happy. Simone's confession had been hard to hear, but it helped Chase make sense of the details of his life. While it sucked to not have Logan—or anyone else—in his life, he had Dak and he had Simone. That was plenty.

He hummed a random song as he plated breakfast.

Arms came around him, and Dak buried his face in Chase's neck. Chase settled into the embrace, reaching back to weave his fingers through Dak's thick hair. He giggled as he realized everything on Dak's body was deliciously thick.

"What's funny?"

"You. I'm so happy, Daddy."

He felt Dak's lips stretch into a smile on his neck. That, coupled with Dak's exhalations, tickled. He laughed again, and Dak spun him around. He crushed Chase in his arms as his lips captured Chase's for a searing kiss. Chase opened, inviting Dak to deepen the kiss, and the alpha did.

Carried away on waves of passion and security, Chase forgot about the food. When Dak broke the kiss, Chase whined.

Dak touched Chase's nose. "None of that, cub. We need fuel, and you need to get home to check on Simone. And I've been called into work."

Protesting wouldn't change anything, so Chase pressed a kiss to Dak's jaw. "Then let's eat, Daddy."

Hours later, Chase hummed as he worked on a car. Flat on his back on a dolly, he enjoyed the contentment that came from being in love and working in a profession he loved.

Finished with his task, he slid out to find Logan lounging against a cabinet full of tools. A bit of Chase's mood soured. "You want something?"

Logan stuck his hands in his pocket and stared at the floor. "I hate this. You and I never fight."

Chase shrugged as if he didn't care, but inside he was dying. Growing up, Logan was the only person who'd been there for him. Though it was a sad comment on his childhood, part of him missed the boy who used to pack two puddings so Chase could have one. "We're not fighting. We'd have to be friends to fight."

At that, Logan squeezed his eyes shut. "Chase, can't we go back to the way it used to be?"

"No." Having the love of a good man, Chase knew his friendship was worth more than Logan was offering.

"It's not just my fathers. It's the whole town."

Chase didn't know what Dak had said to Logan before Logan had left the day before, and he hadn't asked. He figured if he needed to know, Dak would tell him. Now he turned his back on Logan. "I know. You explained that part quite well."

From the frustrated growl behind him, Chase figured that Logan wasn't going to bend. "I didn't want to hurt you. I wanted you to understand."

Whirling, Chase pinned Logan with all the fury in his heart. "So you tried to chase away my boyfriend? Even if you don't want to truly be my friend, why would you pull an asshole move like that?" Then it hit him. "You have a crush on Dak?"

Logan shook his head. "No. I want you to be happy. I just don't want you to be with someone who makes you not want to be friends with me."

Rolling his eyes, Chase went to the computer in the rear of the garage. He punched in the billing codes and work description.

"Chase? Please don't cut me out of your life."

Hardening his heart, Chase didn't capitulate. "You made that decision. I'm not going to let you or anybody else treat me like shit."

It dawned on him that he worked for two men who had no plans to ever pay him more or let their son be friends with him. He knew what he had to do.

He ceased typing, and then he packed up his tools. "Tell your fathers I quit."

Logan pulled on his arm, trying to halt his actions. "Don't quit because of me. Fuck, Chase. I didn't mean to make you quit your job. You love this job. I'll—I'll leave you alone, okay? You don't have to quit."

Yes, he did. He needed to stop working for people who didn't value him as a person. To them, he was just another piece of equipment. He was tired of being used by the Fordlines.

"Goodbye, Logan. Have a nice life."

Dak

The knock on the door came three hours too early to be Chase. Dak shut off the hot water and threw the frozen steaks into the plastic bin. Though he was willing to grill them for Chase, he knew his lover preferred to do the cooking. That suited Dak just fine.

Drying his hands on a towel, Dak crossed the living room and pulled the door open. Standing on the other side was a man he thought he'd never see again.

Loose-fitting jeans and a baggy sweatshirt disguised a slim, solid build. The man pushed back his hood to reveal a shock of red hair and piercing blue eyes. No smile graced his face. He shuffled his feet. "Hey, Dak."

"Hoyt." The man to whom he'd been married for six years stood on his doorstep. When he'd walked out of Dak's life six months ago, Dak had been bereft and plagued by doubts—he should have tried harder, he should have done more to make Hoyt happy.

Now that he was with Chase, he understood nothing he could have done would have made Hoyt happy—or even content. Contentment came from the inside. While others might take it away, they couldn't give it to you.

Hoyt rocked on his heels. "Aren't you going to invite me in?"

Though he didn't want to, Dak also didn't want his neighbors to overhear whatever Hoyt had come to say. He stepped back, allowing enough room for the taller man to enter.

"Thanks." Hoyt unzipped his sweatshirt and tossed it on the sofa. The shirt he wore underneath revealed muscles that were a little bigger than they'd been six months ago.

Dak swallowed the observation. It sounded too much like a come-on. He closed the door. "What do you want?"

Hoyt perched on the edge of the sofa and patted the space next to him. "Sit."

"No, Hoyt. We're not doing this. Say what you came to say, and then leave."

Normally that would be enough for Hoyt to pout and huff out whatever he needed to say. Today it produced a heavy exhalation. "Dak, please. For two minutes, don't be alpha."

Dak didn't have it in him to not be alpha. He chose a chair opposite Hoyt. "Two minutes."

Shades of sadness flashed through Hoyt's eyes. "Early this morning, your fathers passed away."

Stunned, Dak didn't respond.

"Your uncle called me," Hoyt explained. "He didn't know how to contact you."

When his marriage had fallen apart, the bears in Forrest Hills had done everything they could to get them to reconcile. That effort drove Hoyt out first, and then Dak followed once his fathers' health improved. By design, his fathers planned to wait a month before telling family and friends Dak had no plans to return. That was supposed to happen in two days.

"I didn't want to tell you over the phone." Hoyt kept talking. "You deserve better than that." Tears tracked down his cheeks.

"You're lying." It was all Dak could think to say. "They were getting better. They weren't taking medication anymore. I talked to Papa two days ago. He said they were getting stronger every day."

Hoyt's gaze fell. "I'm sorry, Dak. They lied."

White-hot, molten fury had Dak on his feet and closing the distance between him and his ex-husband. Hoyt might be taller, but Dak was bigger and stronger. He snatched Hoyt off the sofa and shook him. "Fuck you, Hoyt. You're lying."

"No." Hoyt didn't struggle in Dak's hold. "I'm sorry. I didn't know you'd left Forrest Hills. I never thought you'd leave." A sob tore from Hoyt. "I'm so sorry, Dak. I loved them, too."

Dak threw Hoyt back on the sofa, and all feeling went out of his body. He sank to the floor. In his head, he was roaring and screaming, railing against the injustice. But in reality, he hugged his arms to his chest and rocked on the floor.

He should have stayed in Forrest Hills. He should have resisted his fathers' efforts to make him leave. They'd framed it as something he needed to do to get over Hoyt and get his career started, but he shouldn't have fallen for it. They'd known the end was near, and they'd deprived him of the chance to be by their sides until the end.

From his first day on duty, he'd told Dad and Papa about Chase. They'd been so happy for him. He'd been planning to take Chase back there one day soon. There had been no reason to hurry. After all, his fathers assured him they were fine. They told him not to visit for three months. They'd told him to give Bear's Cove three months, but he hadn't needed three. It had taken him less than a week to fall for a sexy mechanic who needed someone to set boundaries in his life.

If he had been a good son, he would have visited home anyway. "I'm the worst son ever."

Hoyt stroked Dak's hair. "You were an extraordinary son. It's half the reason I stayed with you so long. You're the most selfless person I know."

"They sent me away. I must not have been that great."

"Don't." Hoyt snuffed out a stream of air. "This is why I came in person. You can't blame yourself. You can't doubt that you were the best son you could possibly be. They loved you beyond all reasoning."

Hoyt swiped a thumb along Dak's cheek, and Dak noticed his face was wet with tears. At that moment, all his reserves crumbled. He buried his face in Hoyt's lap, and his ex held him as they sobbed together.

Time passed, and eventually Dak realized he was kneeling on the floor at his ex-husband's feet. He got up, went into the bathroom, and washed his face. When he emerged, Hoyt was in the kitchen fussing with the frozen steaks in the sink.

"Are you hungry? I could cook these up."

Dak stared at the meat. It seemed like a foreign concept. He shook his head.

Hoyt caught his arm and pulled him close for a hug. It felt so comforting and familiar that Dak didn't resist. He embraced the man who'd left him, and he buried his face in Hoyt's neck. The scent of him was fragrant and familiar, a piece of home that reminded him of his fathers and the life he'd reluctantly left.

The next thing he knew, Hoyt's lips were on his. In a fog of grief, Dak didn't resist the trip back in time to a place where his parents were alive and his life was exactly how he'd expected it to be.

But it was wrong somehow, a memory that shouldn't be relived. When it ended, Hoyt's gaze met his, and Dak looked for evidence his ex felt the same way.

Hoyt smiled, but then the expression fell away. "Hi. I'm Dak's husband. Who might you be?"

Still in Hoyt's arms, Dak turned to see Chase, his form framed by the light in the door. He was early, and he was wearing his mechanic's coveralls.

Chase's dark eyes traveled over Hoyt, his expression revealing nothing about what he was thinking. Wordlessly he took one step back, and then the door closed, the latch clicking softly as it engaged.

Unable to think about what to do next, Dak blinked.

"Was that the repairman?" Hoyt glanced around. "Is your dishwasher broken? It's awfully rude of him to just come in like that."

A car door closed, and an engine started, spurring Dak to action. He hurried outside in time to watch the tail end of Chase's car disappear down the street.

"Dak, go pack a bag. I'll take you home." Hoyt leaned against the doorframe, his arms crossed in a casual pose. "You shouldn't drive in your condition, and give me the number of your repairman. I'll call to reschedule."

The image of his fathers danced in his vision, and words stuck in his throat.

Hoyt set a hand on his shoulder. "Dak, I know I was a bad husband and we had a stagnant marriage, but I'm a halfway decent friend. I'm here for you."

In another lifetime, Dak might have appreciated that. He went inside and grabbed his keys. Brushing past Hoyt, he got in his car.

Hoyt jumped into the passenger seat. "Dak, you seriously shouldn't drive in your condition."

Dak ignored Hoyt. He focused on getting to Chase. Once he found him, the words would come. He'd explain that the divorce was almost final and that he loved Chase. The kiss had been a mistake, and Dak would gladly rectify it. He'd do anything to make it up to Chase.

At Chase's house, he found his lover still in his car. Chase sat in the driver's seat with his head against the backrest and his eyes closed.

Dak opened the door. "Chase, let me explain."

Chase's eyes had opened at the sound of the door. He emerged from the vehicle and faced Dak, his gaze on the driveway and his arms crossed. "Is he your husband?"

"Technically, but—"

"There's no 'but.' You're married or you're not." Though he interrupted, he spoke softly, almost as if adding an afterthought.

"Separated. The divorce will be final next month."

"You didn't look very separated."

Dak wished Chase would be angry—yell, lash out, even shift—but his voice came out quiet and defeated.

"He came to tell me that my fathers died this morning." Dak's voice caught on a sob. This wasn't happening. He couldn't lose everything in one afternoon.

"I'm sorry for your loss." Sympathy flashed in Chase's eyes replacing the dullness there. "You look like you're in good hands."

Chase turned away, but Dak's arms flew out. Before he had a conscious thought, they wrapped around the fragile cub, and he buried his face in his omega's neck. "Please. Chase, I need you."

With his back to Dak's front, Chase struggled against his hold, and a primal part of Dak snapped. Morphing his teeth, he bit into Chase's shoulder. The omega cried out, and he shifted into his bear form, breaking Dak's hold.

Without stopping to admire the sleek brown bear, Dak followed suit. He was larger, and his fur was dark black, almost obsidian.

Chase stood on his hind legs and bellowed a warning that Dak's alpha nature rejected. He leaped, knocking Chase onto his back. The pair rolled, wrestling even though Dak was clearly the dominant bear. It didn't take long for Dak to have the upper hand. This time, his bite subdued the smaller shifter.

Beneath him, Chase stilled, and he shifted back to human form. Dak did as well, which left the two of them naked in the front yard of Chase's house as a pair of cruisers pulled up, lights flashing over their nude forms.

Chase bucked. "Get the fuck off me."

Dak released his teeth from Chase's shoulder. In human form, biting that large of an area made for a painful jaw position. He shifted his weight as he looked around for scraps of clothing to use as cover.

An unzipped sweatshirt landed on his ass. Dak went to hand it to Chase, but Simone was there. Chase wiggled out from under him, and she handed over a pair of sweats.

Cord Bearsmith emerged from one car, and Evan Chillwell stepped out of the other one. Dak wrapped the sweatshirt around his waist, covering up his junk in the front and leaving his ass hanging out for the world to see.

Cord studied him coolly. "Dak, what the hell is going on? Six people called in complaints about excessive noise."

A chill in the air made Dak shiver. Hoyt stepped in, slinging an arm around Dak. "Dak's fathers passed away this morning, and now he's having a disagreement with his...repairman." Hoyt shot Dak a look that said he didn't know what to make of the situation.

Cord knew Hoyt. He'd been at their wedding. "Hoyt, it's been a minute. What are you doing here?"

"Delivering the news. I'm taking Dak home so he can help his brothers get everything settled."

Dak's attention was on Chase. Simone dabbed at the blood on her great-grandson's shoulder, clicking her tongue and talking softly. Chase had donned the sweats, but he didn't seem to hear anything Simone was saying.

Evan steered Chase and Simone into the house. Dak moved to follow, but Cord stopped him with a firm hand on his arm. "Dak, let him go. Simone and Evan will make sure he's okay."

"He's in shock." Dak was finally coming out of the shock that had set in the moment Hoyt had delivered the news. "He needs me."

Hoyt's embrace melted away. "Fuck. I'm sorry, Dak. I'm so clueless. I didn't know."

Cord steered Dak away. "You attacked him."

"I couldn't let him leave. He—he—I had to explain." He'd fucked up on an epic scale, and he didn't know how to fix any of it. Dak ran a hand through his hair. "Let me go to him."

Cord opened the back door to the patrol car. "Why don't you wait inside? It's maybe better than flashing the neighborhood. Hoyt, why don't you wait with him?"

Between Cord and Hoyt, they got Dak into the car. Hoyt sat next to Dak, and the door closed.

Hoyt inhaled. "So, this is what it's like to be arrested. And to think, you used to be so boring."

Dak's gaze remained on Chase's front door. "I'm still boring."

"You're passionate. That's new. When I walked away from you, you waved goodbye and wished me luck. This guy walks in on us kissing, politely leaves, and you go all bear on his ass." Hoyt shook his head. "You never looked at me the way you looked at him. To be fair, I never looked at you that way, either."

In the closed space, Dak was forced to listen. Hoyt had never needed an audience for his incessant chatter, and that hadn't changed.

"Maybe I can explain it to him? I'll tell him I took advantage of you in your weakened state."

At this, Dak sputtered. "I am not weak."

"Whatever. Look, I'm willing to help. I want you to be happy, Dak, and I know that isn't going to happen with me. You're awesome in bed, so I was up for some sex with the ex as a comforting thing, but I didn't know you were involved with someone. That's so unlike you. You're methodical and loyal. It took you four years to seal the deal with me. I honestly didn't expect you'd be hiding the sausage with a hot little repairman so soon."

"Mechanic." Dak's reply came automatically. "Chase is a mechanic, but he can fix anything."

Hoyt's hand closed over Dak's. "Tell me about him."

"No."

"How did you meet?"

Dak swore under his breath. Some things never changed. "I arrested him. Twice. Then he did a checkup on the cruiser. He brought it to my place that evening, and that was it. I fell in love."

"Wow, look at you—whipping out the L-word. That's fantastic, Dak." Hoyt fell blessedly silent for all of three seconds. "This is what your fathers wanted for you. This is why they sent you away. Knowing them the way I do, I know they died secure in the knowledge you had found The One. The last time I saw your dad—when he was helping me

72

load the last of my stuff into the moving van—he said he wished for us both to find the men we were meant to be with."

When Cord opened the door nearly an hour later to let them out, Dak felt as if he'd served a short stretch in prison. Hoyt hadn't stopped babbling the entire time.

Dak took a step in the direction of Chase's front door, but Cord stopped him. "You can't go in there. Chase has decided against pressing charges or even filing a complaint, but he doesn't want you anywhere near him."

That wasn't the news Dak wanted to hear. He tried to shake off Cord's hold, but the older bear's iron grip didn't ease. "Cord, I have to talk to him."

"Give him space, Dak. You did a number on him. It's a good thing he shifted because otherwise you might have caused permanent damage. Simone and Evan put in seventeen stitches as it is."

The full weight of what he'd done hit him. His cub was in pain, both physical and emotional. He'd caused it all, and there was nothing he could do to mitigate the damage. That blow settled in the small piece of his heart left untouched by his fathers' deaths.

Hoyt guided him into his car and drove back to Dak's place, not uttering a single word.

Chapter Ten

Chase

Chase's shoulder itched. As a shifter, he healed quickly. Two days after Dak's attack, Simone pulled out the stitches and only a bite-shaped series of scars was left.

Sheriff Bearsmith sat in Chase's kitchen, sipping the tea Simone had made. Chase nudged the bowl of sugar closer to the sheriff. "You don't have to be nice to me. I'm not suing or pressing charges."

"I'm here to check up on you, son."

Chase rolled his eyes. "Whatever, and don't call me 'son.' It might imply familiarity, and people in this town don't view me as one of their own."

Bearsmith added two heaping teaspoons of sugar to his tea. "You're correct that the residents of Bear's Cove haven't been welcoming to you. After what happened to you, we should have opened our hearts and our minds. But we closed them instead. It was a mistake, one that can't be undone."

Shocked to hear the sheriff speak so plainly, Chase couldn't think of a snarky reply.

"I've transferred Deputy Freeman to the Forrest Hills office. Once he returns from bereavement leave to active duty, he'll be stationed far away from here." Bearsmith sipped his tea. "You won't have to worry about running into him again."

Simone hugged the sheriff. "Thank you. This means a lot to us both."

"I aim to rectify some of the mistakes we've made in this town. Chase will be able to live in peace and safety."

The news should have made him feel better, but the hollow part of his chest where his heart should have resided only ached.

Simone and Sheriff Bearsmith chatted for a bit, and then Bearsmith got to his feet.

He set a hand on Chase's good shoulder. "I'm maybe out of line here, but I want you to know Hoyt told me everything that happened. You should know Dak's never acted like that before. I think losing both of his parents made him go off the deep end. In any event, he's gone."

There it was again, that ache echoing in the void inside him.

After the sheriff left, Chase went into the backyard. Simone had a raised flowerbed, and Chase had built a bench beside it. He sat there and stared at the bare dirt. It was fall, and the bed was littered with withered stalks. It perfectly mirrored the way Chase felt. His heart felt like jerky—dried and encased in scraps that used to be his guts.

A shadow fell over him. "Do you mind if I sit with you?" Logan's voice pulled Chase from the nothingness of his existence. Without waiting for Chase to respond, Logan joined him on the bench.

"Wow. You've come over more after our friendship ended than you ever did when we were supposedly friends."

A soft laugh fell from Logan. "I'm sorry to hear about you and Dak. It's wild, what he did."

It was wild, completely untamed. "I don't want to talk about Dak."

"Okay." Logan rubbed his hands together. "I told my fathers that you were my best friend, and if they couldn't accept it, then we were through."

This penetrated the fog around Chase. "What did they say?"

"They said I was old enough to know what I was doing. And also that I had to move out."

Chase shot a sidelong glance at Logan. "They kicked you out because you want to be friends with me?"

"Pretty much." He pointed to the left. "I'm renting two doors down."

Now he turned his head to peer full-on at his friend. "You did that for me?"

"Yeah. I've been a coward my whole life. You've been the most loyal, best friend a guy could ask for. You've stuck by me even though I was a complete and total dick to you." Logan spread his arms wide. "You stayed with me for a lot of years. You should get to bask in the wonderfulness that is the new me." He followed up with a nervous chuckle that ricocheted from the aluminum siding on the house.

Unable to stay mad at Logan, Chase pulled his friend in for a hug. "You act like a dick again, and we're through."

"Got it." Logan returned the hug. "Also, I got you your job back. My fathers are holding a position for you. You'll even get a raise."

Chase shook his head. "I'm going to open my own repair shop. I'm going to do more than just cars."

"Good for you," Logan said. "I'm working part time at Kizzie's law office."

"Congratulations."

"You want to sue Bear's Cove for your injury, you come see me."

A chuckle escaped Chase. "I'm not suing."

"You have grounds, and they'd settle. You have a shit ton of witnesses who saw him pull you out of your car and attack you."

The small bit of mirth disappeared. "I sent flowers to his fathers' funerals."

Logan sighed. "You are too fucking nice. I mean, I love that you're patient and forgiving, but he tried to kill you."

Dak hadn't intended to hurt Chase—of that, he was certain. He'd been desperate and grieving. And he'd kissed his husband in his kitchen. The bear part of Chase understood what Dak had been doing, but the heartbroken cub couldn't shake the image of his Daddy kissing another man.

Closing his eyes, he confided in his only friend. "I'm pregnant."

"That doesn't mean shit, Chase. You don't have to be with a guy who treats you badly. You deserve so much more than that." Logan smacked him on the good shoulder. "Your baby deserves more than that."

"He wasn't trying to hurt me. He was marking me. If I hadn't struggled, it wouldn't have been so bad."

"Are you fucking listening to yourself?" Logan leaped to his feet and paced behind the bench. "What he did to you—it's not your fault. It's his fault. He was the one who didn't control his temper."

Chase was tired of trying to explain what had happened. Simone didn't understand it at all. "Logan, I don't know how to make you understand. The bite—that was the nature of our relationship. It wasn't the first time he bit me, though it was the bloodiest. I'm mad at him for being married and not telling me. I'm livid that he was kissing someone who wasn't me. It's not the alpha I fear; it's the man who broke my heart who has left me feeling like my world has fallen apart."

It was too fucking late at night for anyone to be pounding on the door. Chase hurried to get it before whoever it was woke Simone.

He jerked the heavy door open to find Dak's husband standing on the other side. He'd recognize the man anywhere. Tall, sexy in an undernourished model way, and sporting thick red curls, Dak's husband was hard to miss. The fucker had the nerve to smile.

"Hi, I'm Hoyt. I'd apologize for waking you up, but I'm not sorry."

Chase was tempted to slam the door in the man's face, but curiosity won out. "What the fuck do you want?"

"To talk. Got a minute?" Hoyt looked Chase up and down.

Chase wasn't wearing a shirt, and so his protruding midsection had no camouflage.

"Damn," Hoyt continued. "Congratulations. I take it Dak doesn't know. There's no way he wouldn't be camped out on your lawn if he did."

"You have five seconds to start talking, or I'm closing the door and calling the sheriff."

"Can I come in? The days are okay, but the nights are chilly." Hoyt wrapped his arms around his torso and shivered dramatically.

Rolling his eyes, Chase opened the screen door. "Five minutes."

"Yay. That's better than five seconds." Hoyt sprawled his long frame on the sofa. "Look, I came because if there's any chance I can put right what I screwed up, I'd like to do that."

Chase sat across from a man who seemed to take up more space than physically possible, and he marveled at the fact that Dak was married to the man. They seemed wholly incompatible.

"So, Dak's uncle called me, looking for Dak because his fathers didn't tell anyone where Dak ran off to. They would've given him shit for leaving, and—believe me—Dak needed to get out of there. Lots of wide-open spaces, but he couldn't spread his wings and fly. So after I left him, Dak's fathers encouraged him to get out and start over." Hoyt paused for a breath and threw a grin in Chase's direction.

Not knowing exactly how to respond, Chase stared.

Needing no encouragement, Hoyt started talking again. "They told me the news, and I knew where Dak had gone because the lawyers needed to know where to send the paperwork. We were getting divorced, you see, so Dak didn't lie. It was final yesterday. We went in front of the judge, and then we went out for a celebratory drink afterward. Dak's a great guy, but we are not suited for each other."

Chase waited while the other man breathed. He should offer water, but he was afraid it would encourage Hoyt to stay longer. "Cut out the bullshit. What do you want?"

"To explain what happened, since you won't listen to Dak. Also, I wanted to tell you that Dak loves you. He never looked at me the way he looked at you, not one time. He's miserable without you."

With a rumbled growl, Chase got to his feet. "Then why was he making out with you?"

Hoyt's face flushed as red as his hair. "That was me. I told him about his fathers. He broke down, and then when he was vulnerable, I kissed him. He was in shock, and he did not participate. After you left, it took him a minute to realize what had happened. He'd just lost his fathers, and then that mistake happened, and it looked like he was losing you." Hoyt cleared his throat. "I didn't know about you. I mean, Dak's not exactly the kind of man who rushes onto the dating scene, so I wasn't expecting him to have a boyfriend. Good for him, though. I mean, good for both of you."

Thunderstruck, Chase stared.

"You should call him, tell him it was a misunderstanding."

But it wasn't. Dak had lied to him about being married. He'd lied by omission, but a lie was a lie, and married was married. Even if the kiss had been accidental, things like that mattered.

Chase got to his feet. "Is that all you came to say?"

For the first time, Hoyt appeared to be at a loss for words. "Yeah. Look, Dak is a good man. You should give him another chance."

Chase showed Hoyt to the door. Thanking him for stopping by would have been the polite thing to say, but Chase's head was spinning too fast for him to know whether he was thankful or not. "No promises."

The next morning, Chase met Logan for their morning jog. "Hoyt stopped by last night."

"Who's Hoyt?" Logan checked his watch because he liked to time their runs.

"Dak's husband. Ex-husband. Apparently the divorce is final."

"What did he want?"

"To tell me I should give Dak another chance. Apparently Hoyt kissed Dak when Dak was shell-shocked about losing his fathers."

Logan grimaced. "I'm still not sure about that guy."

Chase wanted to be. One thing was for sure—the largest roadblocks had been removed. He understood how the kiss had happened, and he was beginning to see why Dak might not have told him about the impending divorce. He'd come to Bear's Cove to escape that part of his life.

Chase watched the pink streaks brighten in the sky. "I'm sure-ish."

Logan finished stretching. "Be sure, Chase. I don't want to have to kill your abusive husband because he's mistreating you. I love you, but I'd rather not spend the rest of my life in prison for you."

After their run, Chase spent a few hours in the small garage behind his house. It wasn't a proper business, but he repaired lawnmowers at home, and he went on house calls to fix appliances. He missed working on cars, but he liked the flexibility of his schedule and the higher paychecks that came with the career change.

He set a hand over his abdomen. Male brown bears had a five-month gestation, which mean he'd have a little cub or a pair of cubs to care for in under three months.

He thought about Dak, and how tender and loving he had been. He was kinky, but not violent. A wave of longing swept over Chase.

He missed his Daddy.

That evening, he stopped by the sheriff's station.

Chapter Eleven

Dak

Four urns held the mixed ashes of his fathers, one each for Dak and his three brothers. Dak stared at them, his mind not processing what he was seeing. Shrouded in the familiar comfort of the living room where he'd grown up, Dak struggled to understand it all.

Ten days had elapsed since Hoyt had reappeared in his life, a grim reaper out to once again ruin everything Dak had built. Dak closed his eyes and fought the urge to blame Hoyt. It wasn't his fault. Dak had fucked up, not Hoyt.

An arm came around his shoulders. One sniff, and Dak identified his brother, Kofi.

"I can't believe they're gone." As the oldest brother, Kofi had been the first to leave Forrest Hills.

Dak couldn't remember a day Dad and Papa hadn't been proud of all four of their cubs. He shook his head as if that would reset his brain. "They kept saying they were okay. They both told me that they were doing better."

Kofi squeezed Dak tighter. "They said the same thing to me, Ashwin, and Cruz. They wanted us to live without worrying about them."

"Selfish," Dak said, an edge to his voice he barely recognized. "I wanted to be here. I took care of them for the past two seasons. What was another month or two?"

"It's okay to be angry," Kofi said. "I am."

Dak peered at his brother. The two of them looked so similar, it was almost like looking in a mirror. "I'm sad. Not only did I lose Dad and Papa, but I fucked up and ruined my relationship with the man I wanted to marry."

Kofi, as oldest, had escaped having an arranged marriage. Dak, ever the people pleaser, had consented to make his parents happy. Kofi didn't say anything, which was how he encouraged Dak to explain. And so Dak spilled every detail of the litany of mistakes he'd made.

When he finished, Kofi frowned. "Chase Longfellow? Cruz was writing thank-you notes for the flowers. He asked if I knew someone by that name. I think your cub sent flowers."

Dak abandoned Kofi, heading to the kitchen where Cruz and Ashwin were working on the notes. "Kofi said there was a note from Chase Longfellow?"

"Yeah." Cruz picked through a pile to his left. At the age of sixteen, Cruz had been struck by wanderlust. He'd begun with weekend hiking trips, and now he spent most of his time in bear form, wandering North America. "Friend of yours? There wasn't a return address."

Dak took the card.

Condolences to the Freeman Family—Chase Longfellow

The message was printed from a computer in a florist's shop. He sank down on an empty chair, the words on the paper blurring. Chase was a sweet man with a heart of gold. He'd sent these flowers because he was sorry for Dak's loss, not because he'd forgiven him.

Cruz watched him carefully. "I almost don't want to give you the letter that arrived today."

Dak's heart thumped painfully. "From Bear's Cove?"

"Yeah. Sheriff's office."

Cord had already called to break the news of his transfer. Dak understood the reasons behind it, but he hated to leave the town he'd adopted. His parents were gone from Forrest Hills, and his brothers no longer lived in the small community. There was nothing for him here. Bear's Cove had become his world.

"Oh. It's just the transfer paperwork." Dak held Chase's card in his hand and went up to his old bedroom. He sat on the bed and stared at the message, desperately wishing it said something else.

Come home.

I miss you.

Fuck you.

Anything was better than the neutral message on the card.

Nothing ever happened in Forrest Hills. Every night was quiet and peaceful. Where the silence had once been soothing, Dak found it oppressive.

His brothers had left days ago, each assuring him that he could stay in the house for as long as he wanted. None of them were eager for the proceeds of an inheritance that had robbed them of their parents.

Dak turned into the driveway of the home where he'd grown up, and he followed the winding path through a thick stand of trees. When he parked, he noted the lights were on inside. He hadn't recalled leaving more than the living room light on, but he could be wrong.

Depression had set in, and he was sometimes forgetful.

He pushed open the door he never bothered to lock.

"Hey. You're home."

The breath left his body the moment he heard Chase's voice. His head whipped around to find the man he loved curled up in Papa's favorite rocking chair. He had a blanket tucked around him against the chill in the air. Dak had turned the heat down before he'd left, reasoning there was no reason to keep it toasty when nobody was there.

Chase's blond hair flopped over his forehead, and the impish grin on his face emphasized his sharp chin and friendly eyes. As he watched, it morphed into something sly and sultry. "Welcome home, Deputy."

Unable to breathe, Dak waited for the punch line. Whatever crap was coming his way, he deserved it.

Chase snagged a handful of colorful candies from the dish next to the chair. Nobody had touched those candies in weeks. Dak hadn't been able to bring himself to throw away Papa's favorite treat.

Chase threw them into his mouth and chewed. Somehow, Dak knew his fathers would have approved.

He indicated a deck of cards on the coffee table. "Want to play poker with me?"

"No." Dak didn't want to play games of any kind. He wanted to take Chase in his arms and never let him go.

Chase leaned forward. "Are you going to come in or stand in the doorway?"

"What are you doing here?" Though he didn't answer Chase's question, he came deeper into the entryway and closed the heavy door. The omega was already cold. He didn't need to let more cold air inside.

Mischief sparkled in Chase's bottomless brown eyes. "Waiting for you."

Dak met the mischief with incredulity. "Why?"

The sparkle fell away, but that didn't dim Chase's inner—or outer—beauty. He folded his hands on his lap. "Hoyt came to see me. He said some things I didn't give you a chance to say."

At a loss, Dak approached. He sank down on edge of the table. Inches separated his hands from Chase's. "What did he say?"

Chase's mood grew somber. "He told me what happened, how he took advantage of you while you were in shock. I'm sorry, Dak. I should have listened to you."

As much as Dak appreciated the lie Hoyt had told on his behalf, he couldn't let it stand. "I let him kiss me. I was equally at fault."

"You weren't in your right mind." Chase's gaze didn't waver. "When I came in, you didn't seem to recognize me. At the time, I thought you were just so wrapped up in him that you'd forgotten about me, but that wasn't true. You were in shock."

Perhaps Chase could forgive the lapse, but it was only the start of Dak's sins. "I attacked you." He swallowed, and his gaze dropped to Chase's shoulder.

Chase sighed. "You did exactly what any alpha would have done to force his omega's submission. That was biology. Next time, I'll be ready."

"Next time?" Dak coughed. "I will never do that again, Chase. Never."

"You know what's funny? This whole incident made me talk to my neighbors, and more importantly, it made them talk to me. They didn't realize we were in a relationship. They thought I'd done something stupid, and you were there to arrest me. Once I explained you were my boyfriend, they understood what had happened." Chase laughed, a cocky sound Dak had sorely missed. "Of course, I didn't, not at first. Being raised by my human great-grandmother means I missed out on learning bear customs and such. It seems you should never turn your back on your alpha when he's riled up. I should have backed away while facing you. Next time, I'll know what to do."

"Next time?" Dak's heart lodged somewhere in the center of his esophagus. "Chase, what are you saying? Do you want to be with me?"

Chase's confidence evaporated. "I do, but there's one more thing."

Dak spread his hands wide. "I'm sorry I didn't tell you I was separated. I meant to, but every time I saw you, I got so wrapped up in being with you that I kept putting it off."

"That's nice, but it's not what I meant." Looking more vulnerable than Dak had ever seen, Chase threw aside the blanket and stood with his hands at his sides.

Dak took in Chase's rounded figure, the swollen midsection that gave away his pregnant condition. Realization set in. "I'm going to be a father?"

"Well, the doctor said it's not bloating from gas."

With a loud whoop, Dak threw his arms around Chase. "Need a kiss, cub."

Chase wound his arms around Dak's neck. "Yes, Daddy."

Dak closed his mouth over Chase's, claiming him with the sweep of his tongue. When they were both breathless, he broke away to trail sucking bites down Chase's neck.

Laughing as if he didn't have a care in the world, Chase threw his head back. "Daddy, how about I heat up some dinner? There's some salmon keeping warm in the oven."

"Later," Dak said. "Right now, I need to claim my omega."

"Is that a marriage proposal?"

"Demand." Dak lifted Chase in his arms and carried him up the stairs. "I demand you marry me. I love you, Chase Longfellow."

"I love you too, Daddy. And I've missed you so very much."

He set Chase on his bed and made tender love to him.

About A. J. Stone

A.J. Stone loves rainbows and bears. Visit https://michelezurloauthor.com/a-j-stone/ for the latest information or follow on Facebook at https://www.facebook.com/AJStoneBearsCove/ to keep up with the newest releases, and feel free to request stories for your favorite Bear's Cove characters.

Reviews let A.J. know you want more!

Bear's Cove Series (MM/MPreg) by A. J. Stone

Dak's Omega
Tanzil's Second Chance
Perfect Blend: Kofi's Omega

Draco International Series (MM/MPreg) by A. J. Stone

Amaricio's Omega Shifter
Koren's Omega Neighbor
Zeke's Reluctant Omega

MM Romance by Nicoline Tiernan

Nexus #1: Tristan's Lover by Nicoline Tiernan
Nexus #2: The Man of His Dreams by Nicoline Tiernan

Sneak Peek at Tanzil's Second Chance (Bear's Cove 2)

"How long are you going to be gone?"

Logan Fordline glanced up from securing his frame pack in the back of his pickup truck. His best friend, Chase Longfellow stood on the other side of the bed, his arms crossed and his bottom lip sticking out. Logan chuffed a laugh. "You won't miss me. Dak will keep you occupied, for sure."

A faint flush stole up Chase's cheeks, and he slapped a hand on the back of his neck. He and Chase had a lot in common, or at least, they used to. The blond pair used to tear up the town on the weekend—partying all night, raising hell, and hooking up with whatever hot alpha caught their interest.

Now Chase was married and pregnant with his first child.

So much had changed in a short time. Now when Logan looked at Chase, all he saw were the differences. Logan's blond hair was sandier, and he had blue eyes to Chase's soft brown ones. Chase had started an appliance repair business that was doing quite well, and Logan chafed under the restrictions of working in a law office.

Chase was finished with the juvenile phase of his life, and he'd made some changes, including setting new parameters for their friendship. No longer would he allow Logan to take him for granted.

Dak's influence had wrought these changes in his best friend, and it had made Logan realize a few things. Namely, he'd been a shitty friend to Chase, and Chase had stuck with him far longer than he deserved. Also law school had not been his idea. He'd gone along with it to please his fathers, and that was the wrong reason to choose a path in life.

In short, Logan was not happy with his life, and he wasn't sure how to change it. One thing was for certain—staying in the same place and doing the same thing wasn't going to make anything happen for him.

Finally, Chase stamped his foot. "Are you going to be back in time for the baby?"

"Yeah, of course. I'm going for a week, maybe two. I just need..." Logan shook his head, uncertain how to explain it. "I need to clear my head. Reconnecting with nature, spending time in bear form—that's what I need right now."

Chase came around the back of the truck and, due to his protruding belly, maneuvered in for a sideways hug. "Be safe. I'm going to miss you."

Though he was tempted to make a remark about how Dak wouldn't leave Chase enough time to miss Logan, he swallowed it down and accepted the sweetness of the sentiment. "I'll miss you too, buddy."

He opened the passenger side of his truck and took out a small gift bag, which he gave to Chase.

Chase eyed it curiously. "For me?"

"Sort of. It's for the baby."

Chase's lower jaw dropped open. "My first baby gift! Can I open it?"

"That's why I'm giving it to you now."

Without waiting a second longer, Chase dug into the bag. He held the gift up between them, his curious gaze going between the brown onesie with a hood that made it look like a bear's ears. It had hand and foot flaps he'd made to resemble bear paws, and the tail was part of the pattern on the back. Logan didn't think anyone would enjoy laying on an actual tail, and he figured it was also a choking or strangulation hazard.

It didn't take Chase long to assemble the puzzle pieces. "You made this?"

Logan shrugged. "You said it would be cute, but I couldn't find anything in the stores. So I got a pattern, and Simone let me use her sewing machine." He didn't add that he'd watched hundreds of hours of sewing videos online, and Simone had helped him with some style issues during his first few runs at making the garment. He was proud of the final product.

A sheen of tears wet Chase's eyes. "It's really good. I mean, you've always loved fashion, but this is really, really good."

A thunk sounded from the other side of the truck. Logan peered over Chase's shoulder to see Dak securing a bag. Dak was a large alpha, broad-shouldered and thickly muscled. His short dark hair grazed his forehead, and his blue eyes smiled at Logan and Chase. He'd recently transferred his sheriff's job back to Bear's Cove because that's where Chase wanted to live.

"What's that?" Logan wasn't sure he wanted to carry more than what could fit on his frame pack. When he shifted, he'd have to stow those things anyway.

"Waterproof matches, bug spray, an axe, and a couple of citronella candles."

Logan wrinkled his nose. "I'm going to be in bear form. I won't need all that."

A husky laugh fell from Dak, who hailed from an outlying area like the one Logan planned to visit. "You'll thank me later."

He came around the truck and hugged both Chase and Logan. Then the trio separated.

"Now, when you get out there, be careful not to wander out of the protected areas. Bears are wanderers at heart, and that sometimes makes it hard to gauge how far out you really are. But if you open your senses, you should have no problem sensing the Wards." Dak drummed his fingers on the edge of the bed and looked toward the sky as he thought. "What else? Oh, avoid interacting with humans. It's bear-hunting season, and humans are assholes most of the time." He shot Chase an apologetic look as he added that addendum. Chase's mother had been human.

Wards were magical spells that kept humans from taking too much notice of the shifter settlements dotting the New England coast. Most humans reacted badly when confronted with the idea of shifters in general, kidnapping them for study or display, or just killing them out of fear or spite.

Chase chewed his lip, and Logan knew his friend was thinking about his mother, and how her own father had killed her rather than let her live as the wife of a bear shifter.

Dak, always sensitive to Chase's emotions, slid an arm around his husband's shoulders and pulled him closer.

"Just be careful," Chase said. He rubbed a hand over his swollen abdomen. "And come back before the baby comes. I know fuck-all about raising kids."

Neither did Logan. He climbed into the cab of his truck and grinned at his friends. "I know you shouldn't swear around them. Maybe start curbing that habit right now?"

With a mighty roar of laughter, Dak said, "We're working on that, Logan. Don't you worry."

Judging from the crimson staining his fair-skinned friend's face, Logan figured a spanking was on the horizon for Chase, but it probably wouldn't be a deterrent. Chase loved a good spanking.

Logan swallowed down a twinge of jealousy. He didn't want Chase or Dak, but he wouldn't mind someone who looked at him the way Dak looked at Chase. That would be nice.